Alpha Captured

International Bestselling Author
SEDONA ASHE
writing as

Darci R. Acula

with Starling Dax

Sensitivity Note
Warning: spoilers below!

Lilou, the FMC, is dying, and she's racing against the clock to finish her life's work.
Beckett, the MC, lost his first mate and is scared to go through that loss again.
While this book has lots of humor, it also has talk of loss and death.
There is dramatic scene where there is a fight that gets violent (not between the couple).
There is a HEA, so you won't be left depressed!
While most of my books involving fated mates are instalove stories, in this book, even though the fated mate bond draws the couple together, it doesn't necessarily make them feel romantic love.

CONTENTS

CHAPTER 1

Lilou

I can do this.

   I can do this.

   I can do this.

I never thought I'd be psyching myself up to— Wait, what was it I was planning to do?

Oh, yeah. Kidnap a mother-freaking alpha.

Maybe if I were a criminal, this would be easier, but I wasn't. Heck, I was a goody two-shoes.

The most criminal thing I'd done in my life was stuffing leftover yeast rolls and honey butter into my purse, even though the buffet didn't allow you to take leftovers home. But come on, it was a far worse crime to toss those fluffy pieces of golden gluten in the trash.

It was that vast experience I was relying on in my

mission to kidnap a powerful alpha werewolf who could tear me to shreds with words… and claws.

I had one thing going for me: I was barely over five-feet tall and a hundred and ten pounds soaking wet. No one looking at me would ever suspect I'd ever do something so capybara-crap crazy.

My size also presented a huge problem, though. I was about to kidnap a guy who was easily six foot and some change.

This would have to go off without a hitch for it to work, and my luck didn't usually roll that way. If this plan had relied on my natural abilities to fall up a flight of stairs or trip over invisible obstacles, I would've nailed it with my eyes closed.

My grade-school friends called me Black-n-Blue Lilou. I'd hated it back then, but now I'd give anything to be teased by a group of friends.

Shaking my head to clear that depressing thought, I clenched my fingers around the steering wheel until the faux leather gave a squeak of protest. I stared out the windshield of my crossover SUV, barely noticing the rain streaking down the glass.

It wasn't too late. I could drive home and curl up in my bed with a book. But I couldn't, not with how much was on the line.

Taking a deep breath, I reminded myself for the hundredth time that I totally had this.

Beckett didn't stand a chance against my wit. Letting go of the steering wheel with one aching hand, I absentmindedly rubbed the bruise on my shin. Okay, maybe it wasn't my wit and charm that would bring him down. But if there was anything I could bet on, it was my absolutely terrible luck.

I was walking proof of Murphy's Law—everything that could go wrong, would go wrong. But now wasn't the time to think about my woes.

No, I needed to go over my plan to kidnap Beckett. Everything had to go perfectly if I had any shot of this working.

As soon as I spotted him, I'd channel my inner gangster. Before he had a chance to react, I'd hide the vibrating silicone gun, which I'd bought at 2 a.m. after reading a rather steamy book, up my sleeve and press it against his side. He'd have no way of knowing it wasn't a real gun. Once I'd shoved him inside my SUV, I would speed away.

Yeah, it was a weak plan. But unfortunately, it was the best I could do given the circumstances. And it had to work.

Clenching my teeth, I tried to ignore the what-if thoughts racing around my head. Thoughts like, what if he simply pulled out of my grasp?

He was a werewolf. A bullet wouldn't kill him, so what if he decided to just turn around and grab my, er, gun? Worse, what if he just turned around and ripped my throat out with his claws?

"Not helpful, Li," I muttered under my breath. "It will be fine. A day or two and this will all be over."

I was still trying to quiet my mind when I caught sight

of Beckett. He was walking in the rain as though he didn't have a care in the world.

His wet, dark green shirt clung to him like a second skin, and his dark jeans appeared soaked as well. Water coursed down the sharp angles of his face, and with a slight flick of his chin, he wiped the water away.

As though he could feel me watching him, he lifted his chin, locking his eyes with mine.

My heart stuttered, and I forced myself to breathe. It was now or never. And while I preferred never, I didn't have a choice. I had to do this.

As Beckett made his way along the sidewalk next to my vehicle, I gathered my resolve and tucked the weapon-of-masturbation inside my oversized coat sleeve. Leaping into action, I threw open my door and slid out onto the wet concrete.

The shockingly cold air wrung a gasp from my lungs as I walked quickly around my SUV. Lunging forward, I grabbed his arm above the elbow with my left hand and shoved the weapon into his back with my right.

"Listen carefully. I have a gun and I'm not afraid to use it," I hissed menacingly. Or it would have been menacing if my voice hadn't wobbled.

Beckett turned his head to gaze calmly over his shoulder at me. He didn't speak say a word, but his arched eyebrow said plenty.

"Don't test me. I'm serious," I growled, pushing him toward my vehicle.

I yanked the passenger door handle, but it refused to open. Probably because it was locked.

Son of a motherless goat! How stupid could I be?

I darted a glance at his face to find him watching me with a slight, wicked smile curving up the corners of his lips.

"Okay. We're going to walk around the car. No funny business, got it?" I tried to seem calm, as though this were totally part of the plan.

He nodded.

Not giving him time to change his mind, I rushed him around the front of my SUV and hit the unlock button. The whole driver's seat was soaked from the rain since I'd left the door open.

Freaking fantastic. I was going to have a wet backside, which would further add to the uncomfortable awkwardness of my evening.

With a sigh, I closed the door and walked him back around to the passenger side. I refused to meet his eyes as I opened the passenger door. Rising up on tiptoe, I placed my hand on top of his head and pushed him down into the seat like I'd seen cops do on crime TV.

I winced at the crack of his head hitting the metal frame. "Oh, my! I'm so sorry! Are you okay?"

Leaning forward, I brushed my fingers on the spot. The gesture was so automatic I couldn't stop myself. His shiny dark hair carried the scent of cedar, rain, and earthy moss.

Suddenly aware I was sniffing his hair like some kind of weirdo, I backed up.

"First time kidnapping someone?" Beckett asked, his forest green eyes sparkling.

I blinked. He was amused by this? I knew I was desperate and crazy, but what was wrong with him?

"How did you know?" Sure, things were off to a rocky start, but he had no way of knowing this was my first time.

Besides, why was being bad at kidnapping such a terrible thing? Being a good kidnapper wasn't exactly something you added to your resume or bragged about at company dinner parties.

Beckett's eyebrows rose nearly to his hairline and I swear I could hear his voice in my head asking if I was serious.

Huffing, I locked his door and closed it, putting the metal and glass firmly between us as he continued to stare at me.

I can do this.

Heck, I'd already done it. Beckett was in my SUV and I was about to drive away with my prisoner.

I rushed around the front of the vehicle and slid into the driver's seat. My heart was slamming against my ribs and I forced my breathing to remain steady.

Shooting Beckett what I hoped was a stone-cold glare, I warned, "I have a knife too, so don't try anything crazy."

He gave me a sideways glance that I couldn't decode. "I wouldn't dream of it."

"Good." I hadn't expected this step of my plan to go so smoothly.

I'd thought he'd put up more of a fight. If someone had

tried to kidnap me, I would have fought like a wildcat. But Beckett made no move to fight me or take control of the situation. If anything, he was acting like I was his rideshare driver.

We'd known each other many years ago, but I was forgettable, so he may not even remember me.

Putting my SUV into gear, I pulled away from the curb and glanced at him again. "Are you comfortable? Do you want me to turn on the heat?"

He tilted his head, studying me with interest. "I'm fine."

But there was no missing the steam rising off his damp clothing, or my own chilly, damp backside.

A shiver traveled through me, and I reached out to turn on the heat. "Well, I'm cold, so I'm sure you must be too."

Beckett gave a slight shake of his head and muttered, "A kidnapper with a heart. Whoever heard of such a thing?"

I risked stealing another look at him. The man was heart-meltingly handsome, but then again, he always had been. If I was being honest, I'd been in awe of werewolves' rugged good looks and powerful bodies for as long as I could remember.

As we pulled onto the freeway, I accelerated quickly to merge with the few cars that were out. In my mind, I cursed the unlucky stars that had led me to this moment where I'd been forced to kidnap an alpha wolf... all thanks to my uncertain future.

Some mythology claimed wolves were cursed, but they had it all wrong. Wolves were blessed.

However, not every full-blooded wolf would shift. The

ones that did were rare and coveted—they were royalty, of sorts.

But I wasn't a wolf. I was something else.

Something truly cursed.

And Beckett was the only one who could save me.

All I needed from him was one simple thing.

A bite.

But it wasn't like I could walk up to him and demand he bite me. That would be insane. Instead, I'd taken the calm, measured solution of… kidnapping him.

It would give me time to plead my case, reason with him, and then hopefully, he'd offer to bite me.

Burning tears blurred my vision at the glaringly obvious flaws in my plan. No matter how this played out, my life was completely screwed up.

If I had any other option, I would have taken it in a heartbeat. The last thing I wanted was to hurt Beckett, but I was running out of time.

"Your pack is going to hunt me down, aren't they?" I asked, working to keep my voice steady. "How long do I have?"

Even in the dark interior, I could see him by the soft glow of the dash and radio screen. The green highlighted his cheekbones, the line of his nose, and his powerful brow.

His glittering green eyes locked on my face, and that same infuriating eyebrow arched again. "Hang on. Didn't you think this through *before* kidnapping me?"

I bit down on my lower lip at the amusement in his

voice. No, I hadn't spent as much time thinking about this part of the plan. And I knew why.

I hadn't actually believed I could get him into my SUV in the first place. But I'd never admit it to him.

"Of course I did. It was just a question," I retorted, lying through my teeth. Remembering I needed to sound in control and commanding, I added, "So answer me."

"Yes, ma'am." Was that a mocking note in his voice? "My pack will notice I'm missing in about two hours when I fail to show up for a scheduled meeting I'm supposed to be speaking at. Then they will start hunting us down."

Crap. I'd have to work faster than I'd expected.

"So, whatever you're planning on doing, you better be quick." Beckett leaned back in the seat as though settling in for a nap.

I peeked at him from the corner of my eye. His expression was serene other than that arrogant, yet adorable, twitch at the corner of his mouth.

Nope. Finding him cute was not part of the plan. My story didn't include love, let alone a happily ever after.

Clenching my teeth together, I focused on the road ahead of me. Large patches of water had accumulated on the road thanks to the downpour, and the SUV drifted slightly, skating on the slick asphalt.

Would his pack be able to track us with all this moisture in the air and on the ground? Maybe if I were lucky, the weather would slow them down, like when people waded through rivers and creeks to avoid dogs tracking their scent.

Except these weren't dogs.

They were wolves, and far smarter than the average dog... although I'd known a few who were far less potty-trained.

CHAPTER 2

Beckett

How long had it been since I'd seen Lilou?

Years.

She was a memory from a past I'd done my best to put behind me. Seeing her should've brought all the dark memories of what I'd lost rushing back. But instead, my heart ached, and I was hit with the realization I'd missed her.

Her deep purple hair glowed in the soft interior lights of her SUV and her eyes stayed locked on the road ahead. The unusual color of her hair almost made her pale gray eyes appear lavender.

Were her eyes shifting colors, or was it just a trick of the light? I tucked that question away to ask another time.

"So, where are we going?" I kept my tone conversational, not wanting to stress her.

Lilou snorted and shot me a quick glance, before focusing back on the rain-slick freeway. "I'm not telling you that!"

I couldn't hold back a smile. "I'll find out, eventually."

The moment I said the words, the scent of her panic and the flustered heat of her body hit my senses. She could cling to the façade of calm, cool, and bad to the bone, but I could smell the truth.

There was another fragrance that was almost completely masked by the others. It was sugary sweet, yet hid a sour scent I couldn't quite place.

I rested my head back against the seat, letting the day's events run through my mind. When I'd woken up that morning, I hadn't expected to be kidnapped by a woman I hadn't seen in nearly a decade. But here we were.

Could I have avoided being kidnapped? Yes. With both hands tied behind my back and wearing a blindfold.

Was I intrigued enough to go along with it, even though I knew she didn't have a gun? Also, yes. Frankly, my life was boring, and this was the most entertaining thing to happen in years.

I didn't know for sure what she'd poked against my back, but I would've smelled gunpowder if she'd had a gun. Instead, when she'd poked me in the back with the soft, round-tipped weapon, I'd smelled only silicone and the faintest hint of... arousal? Which made no sense at all, unless I'd just been kidnapped with a dildo or a massage gun.

I squinted at her, trying to decide if she would've been brash enough to kidnap a werewolf without a real weapon.

Yeah. Lilou was exactly the type of girl to commit a crime with her fantastic plastic lover instead of bringing an actual guy along to act as the muscle.

She'd literally threatened me with a good time.

"So listen, I don't mean to make things awkward, but I really need to use the restroom." It was the truth, but I'd be lying if I said I wasn't looking forward to watching how she would navigate the request.

Even in the low light of the SUV radio and dash lights, I caught the faint pink tinge spreading across her cheeks.

Uncertainty flickered across her face. "Now? Like… right now?"

"I mean, it's not an emergency, but I'd rather not wait too long, you know?" Her dismay made it difficult to hide my amusement.

"Okay, yeah. I'll find somewhere to stop," she mumbled, giving me a double-take when she caught me staring. "What?"

"I've just never had a kidnapper be so thoughtful and worried about my comfort." Lilou was so adorably bad at this. I couldn't help but chuckle.

"Well, how many times have you been kidnapped?" she snapped, more flustered than annoyed.

It was a valid point.

"Alright, this is the first time, but I've seen movies. I'm

pretty sure you're supposed to blindfold me and rough me up," I smirked. "Not caress my head after you banged it on the metal doorframe—"

"That was an accident!" Taking one hand off the wheel, she jabbed her index finger in my direction to punctuate her words.

I couldn't help but grin. She was cute when she was riled up. But before I got the chance to bait her more, red and blue lights began flashing behind us. Lilou checked the rearview mirror and gave a panicked squeak.

"Did you call the cops?" she demanded, her hair flying around her face as she whipped her head to glare at me.

Reaching out, I grabbed the wheel before we could drift into the next lane. Clenching her jaw, Lilou stared hard at the road again. She curled her fingers around the wheel until her knuckles turned white, like she was imagining she was choking someone.

"No, I didn't call the cops." I didn't point out that she would've noticed if I'd made a phone call. "Just pull over."

To my surprise, Lilou didn't argue. Although she did insist on taking my phone. Listening to my voice of reason, she flipped on her blinker and rose in her seat to check her rearview mirror as she crossed the lanes of traffic.

The flashing lights on the vehicle behind us mirrored her motions, pulling off the side of the road and eliminating all hope that they just wanted to get by us to go after someone else.

Part of me found it amusing that she'd kidnapped me

and ended up getting pulled over for seemingly no reason. It was like the universe had it out for her.

There was no way my pack had already figured out I was missing. That meant no one was looking for me, so I had no idea why they were pulling her over. But it was funny all the same.

Lilou came to a halt on the shoulder of the road, and I glanced in the side mirror at the flashing lights on the vehicle behind us.

I studied her, trying to take stock of how she was feeling. Her arms were straight and her hands still white as she gripped the wheel.

She looked at me, wild panic in her eyes. "Please don't say anything."

"Or what? You'll massage me to death with your gun?" I joked.

Her eyes widened, and she shot a quick look between her seat and the console, probably to see if the gun was still hidden. "You knew?"

I shrugged. "Why would I say anything to the cop? You're the one getting pulled over."

She didn't seem to realize I was teasing her and lowered her voice. "Because I kidnapped you, duh."

"Today really isn't your day." I shook my head, feeling almost bad for her, but that didn't stop me from teasing her a bit more. "Please tell me you don't have a warrant out for your arrest. I really don't want to get a reputation for hanging out with criminals and it would be hard to explain to my pack."

"This would be difficult for you to explain?" she huffed, sounding close to tears.

I held up my hands. "Hey, don't get upset with me. I'm the victim here, remember?"

Her hands kneaded the steering wheel, making the faux leather squeak. She was struggling to steady her breathing, breathing that was far harsher than it should've been. That, combined with the unsteady beat of her heart, caused me to take pity on her.

"It'll be okay." I touched her knee, and she trembled, her terror sharp and acrid in the air.

"Maybe now would be a good time to tell me why you kidnapped me?" I asked softly.

She dropped her head, refusing to look at me. "I don't think so. Not yet."

It was the response I'd expected, but not the response I'd hoped for. The officer knocked on the outside of my window and I rolled it down.

"I just want to let you know that my body cam is rolling and I'm on this side for my safety. Do you have any idea why I pulled you over tonight?"

Lilou's terror intensified until she was practically vibrating in the seat next to me.

"No. I don't know, officer." I didn't miss Lilou's sharp intake of breath.

The officer blinked at her. "Are you okay, miss?" He tucked his thumbs into his vest and studied me as if he thought I might be a problem.

Wait a second... Did the cop think *I* might be intimidating *her*?

I was the one who'd been kidnapped. Well, kind of. She was so bad at it that I wasn't sure this met the criteria for a legit abduction, but technically, she was the one breaking the law. I was just along for the ride.

"I'm fine, just scared because I've never been pulled over before." Lilou reached into her pocket. "Here's my license. Registration and insurance are in the glove box."

She leaned over me to open the compartment. Lilou's gorgeous body brushed against my thigh and her heat sank through my jeans and into my skin. Something stirred in my chest—something that I'd never expected to feel again.

After rifling around for a minute, she finally pulled out the documents and offered them to the officer, who hadn't taken his eyes off me. He slowly took them and headed back to his car.

"He thinks I'm kidnapping you," I whispered.

"Oh, wonderful!" She gave a half-hiccup, half giggle.

"No, it's not. How is that wonderful?" I hissed.

She glanced at me, relief swirling in her big gray eyes. "If he thinks you kidnapped me, it means he doesn't think I could be a threat to you."

"Well, that is some sexist, back-arse-ward bologna. You kidnapped me with a gun. Doesn't that count for something?" I growled.

Lilou snorted. "A massage gun."

I narrowed my eyes at her. "Oh! It counted as a gun

when you wanted it to, but now it doesn't count as a weapon? It won't kill me, but it's the principle of the thing."

She rolled her lip into her mouth and I could swear she was trying not to laugh. Despite my annoyance, I was relieved her breathing had calmed and her heart had found its rhythm again.

A moment later, the cop reappeared at the window, offering Lilou her documents. "You have a taillight out, miss."

"Oh, I had no idea!" Lilou's relief was palpable, and a smile curved her lips. "I'll get that fixed as soon as possible, officer."

The officer nodded. "Please do. It's a hazard, especially in this kind of weather." He motioned to the pouring rain.

"Thank you, officer. I'll pull off at the next exit and find an auto parts store. Someone has to visit the little boy's room anyway," she replied with a grin.

I couldn't remember ever being so offended by a bathroom break in my life. If I hadn't been distracted by her hand squeezing my knee and sending electricity sizzling through me, I might have said something.

The cop eyed me with a tight, calculating smile I didn't appreciate, and patted the windowsill. "Well, drive safe. The weather is only supposed to get worse."

I sensed him hesitating just a moment too long, as if waiting for some sign from her that she needed his help. When she only continued to smile up at him, he tipped his hat and walked back to his car.

"I'm glad that's over." She blew out a breath.

I blinked at her.

She hesitated, catching her bottom lip between her teeth. "Why didn't you tell him I kidnapped you?"

That was the million-dollar question. The honest answer was I hadn't been this entertained in years. Just like turning the pages of a good book to see what happens in the next chapter, I found myself wanting to know where this was going... and what she was up to. But I wasn't about to tell her that.

"And miss out on the pure comedy that is your kidnapping attempt? Not a chance." I winked, and her eyebrows scrunched together cutely over her nose. "Who knows? I might turn this into a book, or a play!"

"Rude," she scowled at me. "I think I'll stop by the auto parts store first, just so you have to wait longer to go to the bathroom."

There was no holding back my smirk as she pulled out onto the open road once more.

CHAPTER 3
Lilou

I couldn't believe the nerve of this man.

The sparkle of amusement in his eyes, and the way he was pressing his lips together, told me he was trying not to laugh.

It made me like him.

I shouldn't, but I did.

He was taking what was a very stressful situation for me —my first time kidnapping someone—and was turning it into something almost fun. It was weird, but it almost felt like we were on a date, rather than in the middle of a kidnapping.

Not that I had a lot of kidnapping experience. I'd done this exactly one time… this time. Still, I didn't think we were supposed to be smiling and having fun together.

Alpha wolves were notoriously difficult, and never in a million years would I have expected to click with one. Especially this one.

Beckett was one of the most difficult wolves to get close to. He was known for being cold, calculating, and willing to make the hard choices no one else wanted to make.

I'd compiled these details as part of my research, so that I'd know what to expect while holding him hostage.

Getting caught was a given in my plan. There was no way around it. No one could keep an alpha captive indefinitely, and his pack would find us. I'd needed to know how long I had before that happened.

Plus, I was curious what would happen once I'd been dragged back to his pack, and they made an example of me. My research taught me that my punishment would be appropriate. Beckett made fair decisions, but he wasn't known for being merciful.

So who the heck was this man with the beautiful eyes and sense of humor sitting in my passenger seat? I snuck a peek at him from the corner of my eye.

Maybe the wolf I'd meant to kidnap had already been taken... by aliens. Because Beckett couldn't be the one making me want to smile when I should be crapping my pants over how badly my plan was going.

"Why are you looking at me like that?" Beckett's words were unexpectedly soft, almost velvety as they fell from his kissable lips.

My heart lurched. Surely I hadn't been looking at his lips thinking about how kissable they would be.

Of course not.

Because that would be insane.

"You're not what I expected." The truth slipped out, and I immediately wished I could pull the words back in.

"Is that so?" His eyes crinkled at the corners and a smile flirted around the edge of his mouth.

"No. I mean, yes," I answered, completely flustered.

Sagging back into my seat, I stared out the window, trying to figure out my next step.

All my careful planning had fallen apart. At that point, I wasn't sure how to navigate the situation I was in. Maybe I should just call it quits, because how on earth could I make sure he wouldn't escape during his bathroom break?

I'd seen enough movies with a kidnapping plot to know how this worked. In fact, I'd streamed dozens of them the last few months, you know, for research. Once you got in the bathroom, you simply squeezed out the window and ran until you could blend into a crowd. Then you asked for a phone, or ducked into another shop to hide.

Basically, the kidnapped person was outta there before the dumb kidnapper figured out they were missing. And let's face it, I was incredibly bad at kidnapping. There were a lot of things I was bad at, but I really sucked at this. Heck, if they gave out awards for crimes, they wouldn't even have given me a participation trophy.

Blowing out a long sigh, I turned into the auto parts store's parking lot and eyed Beckett. There was no way I could leave him in the car, so he was going to have to go with me. Beckett didn't raise a fuss, and we headed inside and straight to the counter.

"How can I help, bro?" The clerk focused on Beckett, dismissing me as though I didn't exist. *Jerk.*

Beckett took it in stride. "I've got a taillight out. Can you look up the part for me?"

I didn't need him to do that. They probably thought I was just a dumb girl who didn't know anything about vehicles. I bet they'd both be shocked to learn I changed my oil myself.

Clearing my throat, I rattled off the make and model of my vehicle, and waited while the guy looked it up. To his credit, Beckett stepped aside, clearly aware I wanted to be in charge here.

"Right. The bulb is on that wall back there." The guy seemed bored as he gestured in the general direction of the bulb.

Beckett followed without a word as I moved to the back of the store and grabbed the correct package off the wall. Marching back to the counter, I placed the small package on the counter and took out my card to pay. The cashier ran my card, then handed it back to me with the receipt.

"Have a nice night." He nodded at Beckett, still acting like I didn't exist, and I resisted the urge to make a childish face at him as I took my part and left.

At the SUV, I pushed the button for the lift gate and stared at the light.

It couldn't be *that* hard. I spotted the place where I could unscrew a couple of bolts and grabbed my little tool bag.

"Nifty bag. Need help?" Beckett asked, leaning against the vehicle.

"Nope. Feel free to just stand there and look pretty." I sarcastically batted my eyelashes before taking out my screwdriver.

Focusing on the screws, I took out one, then the other, and wiggled the blown light free. I sensed Beckett watching me and raised my gaze to meet his stare.

My breath froze in my lungs. The warmth in his eyes caused a fuzzy excitement to bubble up in my belly and chest.

No, no, no. I couldn't let myself be attracted to him.

Beckett reached out and plucked the light housing from my hand. He was so close that the heat radiating from him was warming my blood. I swallowed hard, fighting the urge to take a step back.

Pinned between him and my SUV, I couldn't help but feel trapped. To my surprise, rather than feeling afraid, his closeness caused my heart to race and an unfamiliar hunger to flare in my belly.

"I know you can do this without my help," he said in a low, husky voice as his fingers expertly twisted the housing to remove the socket the bulb rested in, "but I don't like being useless."

Every joke and snappy comeback drained from my body. Taking a shaky breath, I pushed the new bulb into place.

"Thank you." I whispered the words under my breath, and his eyes narrowed.

Beckett's gaze traced my lips before darting back to mine. "You're welcome."

I never thought replacing a taillight could turn into such a sexy moment, and I was one of those women who watched food porn videos. The type where hot guys made delicious desserts videos that made me wish I could be the next ingredient.

With his body so close to mine, all I could think about was the size of his large calloused hands, the heat in his expression... and that I shouldn't be thinking thoughts like these.

Needing to diffuse the situation, I inhaled deeply and let the breath out slowly.

I dropped my eyes to the light as he fit it back into place. "Where did you learn to do these things?"

"Family. We all help and teach every chance we get." His words punctured my heart like an arrow.

I didn't have a family to fall back on.

"And you?" he asked.

"Mostly through online videos."

"There's nothing wrong with that." His voice was gentle and the backs of my eyes burned.

"I imagine it's important for the pack to help each other." I allowed myself to wonder, for just a second, what it would feel like to have a family, support, and love.

Giving my head a shake, I tried to clear my mind. I needed to stop torturing myself unless I wanted to risk breaking down in front of him. With tears stinging my eyes and the aching sensation in my throat, I knew a breakdown was imminent.

"It is." His hand grazed mine as he took the screwdriver from me.

Unable to meet his gaze, I picked up the screw. Putting the metal into the hole, I twisted it a few times before he took over with the screwdriver. He was a wolf, and the fact he'd no doubt sensed my sadness made me wish I could become invisible.

"Want me to go press the brake?" Beckett asked.

I nodded, hoping a new bulb was all that was needed to fix the light. A moment later, the engine turned over, and the light came on. My flash of excitement over the repaired light was quickly dashed as the vehicle pulled forward and away from me.

Beckett was stealing my SUV.

My heart thundered against my ribcage and I sprinted after him. How could I have been so stupid?

He stopped at the road, then pulled out, driving toward the gas station at the corner. I watched in shock as he pulled into the gas station. Parking outside the little store, he hurried inside, only pausing to shake the keys at me and grin.

I raced down the sidewalk. If he hadn't distracted me with his gorgeous body, I wouldn't have been such an idiot. I should've known he'd try to escape, but I hadn't thought he'd take my vehicle!

Jogging into the gas station, I looked around for him, but Beckett was nowhere to be seen.

"Hey, did a tall guy just come in here?" I asked the attendant, who nodded and gestured toward the bathroom.

I rushed over. He had my keys, so if there was a window in there, he could take my SUV and disappear forever.

"He hasn't come out yet?" I asked, and the attendant shook his head, his brows furrowing like I'd lost my mind.

Maybe I had. But who could blame me under the circumstances?

To MY SURPRISE, Beckett did not climb out the bathroom window. I glanced at him as he walked beside me out of the gas station. Reaching the SUV, he held up the keys, and I snatched them out of his hand in a swift motion. The corners of his mouth twitched as though he were trying to keep from laughing, but I ignored him and made my way to the driver's seat.

I eyed him warily, waiting to see what he would do. Like a good captive, he walked around and climbed into the passenger side. This had to be the most upside-down kidnapping ever if my captive was climbing into my vehicle of his own free will.

It made no sense. I tried to hang onto my anger over him ditching me at the parts store, but it was an effort in futility. After all, when you had to go, you had to go, right?

Beckett hadn't run off when he'd had the chance, so if escaping was his plan, he'd failed spectacularly. And he definitely should've been trying to get away from me, yet he wasn't.

In fact, he almost seemed delighted to be my captive, which made this whole situation even weirder. Maybe he knew his pack was already tracking us and that was where Beckett's unbothered attitude was coming from.

Clearing my thoughts, I focused on the one thing I knew for sure: I needed to get my head back in the game. Beckett had me all twisted up inside, and that could be a problem.

After all, I wasn't doing this for me. There were too many lives at stake for me to get distracted.

Once inside, our gazes met over the center console and I cleared my throat. "Are you hungry?"

"All right. Fess up." Beckett's eyes sparkled. "This has to be your first time kidnapping someone, right?"

I shoved the keys into the ignition before crossing my arms. "It's your first time being kidnapped and you've only seen this stuff on TV. So maybe this is how real kidnappers handle things! Besides, I don't want you to starve to death... or worse, get hangry."

He arched a dark eyebrow at me. "Getting hangry is worse than dying? Noted."

I fought the urge to laugh, but the next words from his lips had all humor fading like the air had been let out of a balloon.

"So will kidnapping me be worth it when it comes time for you to face the music? Let's be real. The cops, my pack, and the world aren't going to look kindly on you once this gets out." His voice was soft, almost pitying. "What could you possibly hope to gain from this?"

I froze, unable to form a response. In my mind's eye, I remembered writing out long lists in my journal, detailing the plan and how I hoped it would conclude, relying heavily on my movie research. I'd known my hopes were unrealistic, and I'd carefully avoided thinking about the uncomfortable truth of how this would end for me.

Kidnapping anyone was bad, but I'd spent way too much of my life working long hours, just to lose all the progress I'd made. I was in a darned if I did, and darned if I didn't situation.

All because life wasn't fair, and it definitely wasn't kind.

My throat tightened, and I blinked hard against the sting of tears.

I'm not going to cry in front of Beckett, I repeated like a mantra in my mind, refusing to be vulnerable.

Opening my mouth, I tried to come up with the right words on the fly. "It sounds like you're already getting hangry. We definitely need to stop for food."

I was more than a little relieved that I sounded composed, as though unbothered by his words. Meanwhile, my guts were tying themselves in knots—and not in the warm and fuzzy way they had earlier.

In the blink of an eye, he'd reminded me there would be no happy ending for me when this was over. Pushing aside my depressing thoughts, I focused my attention on driving.

"I didn't mean to upset you," Beckett whispered, no doubt picking up on my dark mood.

But I barely heard him. In my mind, I was a million miles away, thinking about the possibility of being arrested. I was doing this because I felt it was justified, since it was for the greater good. Besides, what was more justifiable than saving countless lives?

However, that excuse wasn't likely to save my bacon when I was arrested. Unfortunately, I didn't have the luxury of time, which was needed when things went through the proper channels. The only upside was that I wouldn't be alive long enough to go through the stress of a trial.

"I remember you, you know."

Like magic, Beckett's words snapped me out of my faraway thoughts.

"No you don't." My response sounded defensive even to my own ears.

There was no way he remembered me. We'd crossed paths so long ago and I was a different person now, in every possible way.

"Lilou. You were best friends with..." I heard his sharp intake of breath and understood it immediately.

Saying her name brought him the same pain it brought me.

He does remember me.

Clenching my teeth, I gripped the steering wheel tighter. I'd hoped he'd forgotten me. After all, I'd played such an insignificant role in his life and I'd only known him through her. And she'd been gone for so many years now.

I'd assumed I was forgettable enough that Beckett

would've long since forgotten who I was and that I existed. Maybe it had been foolish thinking on my part since I'd been best friends with the most important person in his life.

"How about here?" I pulled into the parking lot of a chicken place I didn't frequent, but had heard good things about.

My stomach churned, and I no longer cared in the least about eating. But I desperately wanted to shut him up before he said something that broke the dam and I burst into tears.

Beckett studied me. "Sure, I guess."

"What do you want to eat?" I asked, rolling down my window in front of the drive-thru speaker.

"I've never eaten here, so I don't know what to order." He leaned over the console, peering out my window to see the menu board.

His shoulder brushed against me, causing butterflies to beat around inside my already quivering stomach. If this was a date, I would've leaned forward to steal a quick kiss from the gorgeous wolf.

But it wasn't a date, and I turned my attention to the board, and the chicken noodle soup caught my eye. Maybe I could eat that without upsetting my stomach.

"I'm getting soup."

"That sounds good. I'll eat that too."

"Surely you eat more than soup." I shot him a quizzical glance.

His eyebrows lifted. "Are you commenting on my weight or my physique?"

"No, of course not." I blushed. "You're a wolf, and you have a higher caloric need. That's just science."

Wolves needed a minimum of five thousand calories per day thanks to their insanely fast metabolism. A bowl of soup wasn't going to keep him full very long.

He chuckled, letting me know he'd been joking.

I blew out a weak laugh. "Sorry. I need to loosen up, huh?"

As someone who'd been teased and told I needed to eat a burger because of my slim frame, I was a bit sensitive when it came to body shaming. I'd never want to hurt anyone, unintentionally or otherwise.

"Maybe a little." Beckett grinned at me.

Breaking eye contact, I pulled forward and ordered the two soups and a couple extra sandwiches to make sure he'd have ample snacks.

After taking my order and being directed to pull forward, I took a breath. "When we get where we're going—"

"Which is where?" he asked, interrupting me with an expectant expression.

Did he think I was born yesterday? "I'm not going to tell you that. Not yet."

I rummaged around in my purse, searching for my credit card. Locating it, I passed the card to the person at the window and took the two containers they'd handed to me. With my hands full, I wasn't sure where to sit the soups so I could get the rest of the food.

I handed Beckett one of the Styrofoam soup containers

and turned to grab the takeout bag from the window. It was as I held out the bag toward Beckett that I felt it slipping from my right hand and tightened my grip.

Reflexively, my left hand copied the movement, and I squeezed the soup container too. The Styrofoam container broke, sloshing hot soup over my hand and pouring into his lap.

"Ahh!" I yelped.

Beckett tried to push himself off the seat as if that would help him escape the hot food that had already soaked his lap. Grabbing a handful of napkins from the bag, I stammered my apologies and began rubbing at his wrecked pants with the napkins.

"Oh, crap! I'm so sorry! I have no idea how that happened."

Alternating between blotting and then rubbing at the soup, I sent bits of noodles, chicken, and carrots onto the floor. I didn't immediately notice the odd glance he was giving me, and then it took another second to realize what I was rubbing.

Um... *him.*

His, uh, yeah.

That part.

Heat seared my cheeks, and a flush traveled from my head to toes.

"Oh, uh... sorry?" I squeaked, wishing I could pretend that hadn't just happened.

My heart slammed hard against my chest wall, and blood pounded in my ears as the world began to go dark at the edges. Was it possible to pass out from embarrassment? Or had I simply pushed my body's limits too far that day, both physically and emotionally?

How could I ever look him in the eye again?

"I'll, uh… get you a new soup." The person at the window coughed, and I realized they'd witnessed everything.

Me spilling the soup.

Me rubbing Beckett… *down there.*

I doubted the moment could get any worse.

Beckett turned to stare out his window, avoiding even looking in my general direction. What was he thinking right now?

Hopefully he didn't think it had been a ploy to get my hands on his…

"Wiener?"

"What?" I half-shouted, half-wheezed, and clutched my chest. My eyes shot to the window where the worker blinked at me, holding up a brown paper bag.

"I'm waiting for soup," I croaked, wondering if the entire universe was laughing at me right now.

"Oh! Wrong order. Must be for the car behind you." The person gestured to the vehicle behind me, and I fought the urge to shrink down in my seat.I swear that if I wasn't already dying, I'd be dying from embarrassment.

CHAPTER 4

Beckett

I didn't think my kidnapping misadventures could have become any more amusing, but Lilou proved me wrong.

Things took a weird turn when hot soup dumped in my lap and then got even weirder when my adorable captor accidentally groped me.

As soon as she'd realized where she had been aggressively rubbing, she'd turned a red that made it seem she'd been the one burned. The sharp scent of embarrassment rolled off her in waves, like the warning on the wind before rain came. If I wasn't worried about laughing and causing her to snap, I might have tried to comfort her.

Knowing I'd burst out laughing if I looked in her direction, I kept my gaze focused out the window. I clung to the door handle like a cat clinging to a shower curtain so it didn't get wet. Except I was already wet.

The most confusing part of the whole situation was how quickly my body had responded to her innocent touch, and how a small part of me had wanted to stop her rambling apologies with a kiss.

Wolves got one mate. I'd found mine, and she had already passed from this world to the next. So why was my body, and wolf, responding to her touch?

I should have been angry with her for disrespecting me with this farce of a kidnapping. If anyone else had tried this, my wolf would've ripped the door off their vehicle and I would've dragged the offender back to my pack.

But instead of getting away from my novice kidnapper, I wanted to pull her onto my lap and bury my face in her hair. I wanted her to wrap her fingers around the hard length she'd roused with her cleaning efforts. Mostly, I wanted to hold her tight, breathing in her scent and reassuring her I'd protect her from whatever had her so desperate that she'd abduct an alpha.

Turning my head a fraction, I glanced at her from the corner of my eye. Lilou's cheeks were still bright red and I could practically see the steam coming from her ears thanks to her internal fuming.

Lilou broke the silence. "I need to stop."

"Okay." At this point, I was just along for the ride and hoped I wouldn't have to wait long for the answers I wanted.

I needed to get those answers and then get away from her before my pack figured out she had me. Otherwise, what was I going to do when Oliver, my right-hand wolf, dragged Lilou through the pack of wolves and threw her at my feet, demanding she pay for her crime?

Oliver was my best friend, and I knew him well enough to know he'd want to keep up appearances. Allowing Lilou to get away with this—the ultimate crime against the pack—would tell my pack members, and other packs, that they could disrespect me as they pleased because I was too soft-hearted and weak to punish them for it.

Closing my eyes, I blew out a long sigh. If my pack realized this was a kidnapping, I'd be forced to make an example of her, and I didn't want that. But I couldn't leave until I had answers and knew why she'd been desperate enough to attempt this farce of a kidnapping.

Deep down, I knew that wasn't the only reason I wasn't in a hurry to leave.

I like the way I feel being around her.

Strange as the thought was, it was as though life was less heavy and a little less dark since she'd shoved me inside her SUV.

Or maybe it wasn't her presence at all. Maybe it was just that this outing was providing a welcome distraction and the weight of responsibility would come crashing right back down on my shoulders once I returned to my pack.

Lilou pulled into a motel that sat far outside town and turned off the engine.

She stared, unseeing, through the windshield as she mulled something over. "Come with me."

Ah. That made sense. Lilou had needed to choose between the lesser of two evils. She either had to leave me in the vehicle and trust that I wouldn't bolt, or she had to drag me along and hope I didn't cause a scene.

Apparently, she'd rather drag me along. That was fine by me.

Her SUV smelled like her, and with each breath I drew in, it felt as though my wolf was becoming a tad more attached. I needed some fresh air. Climbing out, I fell into step beside her, sucking in lungfuls of the cool night air and inhaling the fragrances of the new location.

I stepped in front of her and opened the lobby door. Ushering her through with a flourish, I followed her inside as she made her way to the front desk.

"I have a reservation for a room with two queen beds." She fumbled with her wallet and pulled out cash.

The clerk gave her a bored look, then studied me for a minute. When he finished his once-over, he began clicking at the keyboard with the speed of a sloth.

Ducking my head, I whispered in Lilou's ear, "You might want to tell him the reservation was for tonight, because if he goes any slower, we won't get our room until tomorrow night."

She sucked in her cheeks to keep from giggling and my chest warmed with pride at making her smile.

Finally, the guy ran a tired hand through his shaggy

blond hair with one hand and sighed loudly. "I've got you in room six."

He pulled out a key from beneath the counter.

Lilou took the key and handed over the cash. It took him an excruciatingly long time to give her change, but eventually she led me toward the door.

Pausing just before we reached it, she half-turned toward the guy again. "Just confirming, there are two queen beds, right?" Her eyes narrowed as though she were suspicious.

"You got it, boss." The guy clicked his tongue as he pointed and shot her a wink.

"That was weird," Lilou mumbled under her breath, curling her arm around mine as we left the lobby.

My chest warmed yet again at the casualness of her gesture. It showed her comfort level with me, and I doubted she was even aware of what she was doing.

We made our way down the cracked pavement sidewalk until we reached our room. Releasing my arm, Lilou inserted the key into the lock and opened the door.

Her angry hiss as she entered let me know something wasn't right. Stepping inside, I was greeted by the sight of not two beds... but one king-sized bed.

I rubbed my hand on the back of my neck and pressed my lips together, trying to hide my amusement. Lilou didn't just have bad luck, she had straight-up rotten luck when it came to this kidnapping, and I couldn't help but wonder what she was going to do now.

My question was answered when she stormed from the room, dragging me along behind her. She came to an abrupt halt at the lobby door. Taped to the glass was an *out to lunch* sign, despite the late hour.

"You have got to be kidding me," Lilou snarled, pulling out her phone. "I made reservations for two queen beds! They must have given someone my room!"

Tapping in the motel's number, she held it up to her ear and angrily tapped her foot on the pavement. It rang for several long minutes before she gave up and ended the call.

Putting both hands to her head, she massaged her forehead, seemingly unsure of what to do.

"We should probably go back to the room and figure this out. The longer we stand here, the higher chance someone will recognize me and blow your whole kidnapping plan. Didn't you read *Kidnapping 101* before you grabbed me?" I teased, unable to resist the desire to ease her stress.

"No. But I watched 101 kidnapping movies," Lilou answered with confidence.

You have got to be kidding me.

Shaking my head, I made my way back to the room, with Lilou following along behind me.

"We can make this work," I assured her as she stopped beside me.

What was wrong with me? Why should I care about her feelings? Why did I want to see her smile?

Turning slowly, I took in the small room. The outside had been slightly run down, so I found myself somewhat surprised that the inside was nice. Dark wood panels went halfway up the walls before giving way to clean white drywall that traveled up to the dark wooden molding.

Lilou remained quiet, chewing her lip as she too studied the room.

Hoping to ease her worry, I added, "Then again, maybe not. Especially with how hard it was for you to keep your hands off me in the vehicle."

She glared up at me. "I was cleaning up my mess, not feeling you up!"

I held back my chuckle. Her embarrassment was throwing her off balance, and it made her even more adorable... like an angry kitten. I could practically feel my wolf wagging his tail, wanting me to keep pushing her buttons—in a nice way, of course.

"But, I mean, think about it. You manhandled me in the drive-thru while we had an audience and now we're sharing a hotel room. I'd say as far as the world is concerned, we're practically married at this point," I said, digging in as I stepped toward her.

Her throat shifted as she swallowed hard. "*Practically married* because I tried to clean soup off your lap?"

"Is that what it's called nowadays?" I teased.

Lilou snorted. "I have no idea what other people do or say. Dating isn't something I do."

"No, you just enjoy kinky voyeurism stuff on first dates, like you did in the drive-thru?"

Her cheeks flared red. "We're not talking about that."

"I sure would like to," I purred, unable to hold back my grin.

It wouldn't be a big deal for me to sleep on the floor, but I refused to make the offer. Watching her muddle through this ridiculous kidnapping plan was the best entertainment I'd experienced in years.

"I can't with you right now. I'm going to take a shower." She spread her fingers on her forehead and began rubbing frantic circles on her temple.

She was going to trust me to stay put?

"Take your time. I can sit and watch TV or something," I said with as much innocence as I could muster up.

Her spine stiffened. "Absolutely not."

Riffling through her bag, she pulled out a set of silver handcuffs.

Disbelief washed through me. "Really? After everything, you still think I'd run? I've been a good boy."

Lilou shot me a look that said, *yeah right*. Taking the cuffs, she snagged my wrist and studied the room. She seemed unsure of where to cuff me, and a quick scan of the small space told her there were exactly zero good options.

Sighing, she pulled me toward the bathroom. The options there weren't much better. There was a hand towel rack at the sink or the bath towel rack on the wall, neither of which looked too sturdy.

Finally, her eyes drifted upwards and her expression brightened.

"Oh, no," I growled. "Surely, you're not about to—"

She pulled me forward and lifted my arm with the silver

cuff attached. With a click, she hooked the other end of the cuffs on the thick metal shower rod that was bolted into the walls.

Stepping back, she arched an eyebrow and admired her handiwork.

"You are into some kinky stuff, kitten," I rumbled, enjoying the way her lips parted and her quick intake of breath at my low tone. "If you wanted me to watch you bathe, you could have just told me. The cuffs weren't necessary."

"I didn't bring you in here to watch me!" she squeaked. "Turn around, please. And no peeking!"

I could have refused just to mess with her, but I decided to go along with it. While I was the one currently connected to a shower rod, she'd had a pretty rough day... not to mention it was going to get even worse when my pack showed up.

"So you didn't trust me to stay put in the room, but you trust me not to sneak a look?" I teased as I turned away from her.

The whisper of fabric being removed from her body was followed by the muffled thud as her clothing dropped to the floor. Unable to fight the urge to see her, I glanced over my shoulder.

A long scar ran down her arm, from her elbow almost to her wrist. I caught sight of the distinct suture marks where the wound had been sewn closed. She'd been through something traumatic.

Lilou realized I was peeking and let out a strangled

noise. "Turn around, mister! Peek again and I'll blindfold you."

Facing the wall again, I couldn't help but wonder if it was an accident, an attack, or maybe something to do with her health.

She said nothing more about my disobedience, and a moment later, turned on the water. The sound of water splashing against skin told me she'd stepped beneath the shower's spray.

Her scent shifted with a suddenness that caused every hair on my body to lift in alarm. Tilting my head, I tried to catch more of her fragrance, trying to figure out what was going on.

Lilou's pulse slowed and her breathing quickened. Something wasn't right.

Risking her wrath, I turned just in time to see her grip the shower curtain and her eyes roll back. Her muscles went slack, and she toppled toward the back wall of the shower, yanking the shower curtain from the rings one by one as she fell.

Jerking forward, I wrapped my free arm around her waist before she could hit the tub floor. She went limp against my chest, unmoving and not making a sound.

With one arm above my head, still attached by hand-cuffs to the shower rod, and the other arm wrapped around her slick body to keep her from falling, I strained, trying to hear her pulse.

My own heart stood still, not daring to beat until I caught the soft double thud of her heart beating.

She wasn't dead.

Relief washed through me and I closed my eyes for a minute, working to calm my wolf.

But my rush of gratefulness abruptly turned to confusion as her scent filled my lungs. Where did I recognize the scent from?

CHAPTER 5

Lilou

Jolting awake, I sat bolt upright in bed and tried to clear the confusion from my mind. The last thing I remembered was being in the shower. Now I was in bed with no memory of how I got there.

What about Beckett? Had he escaped? My stomach churned as I searched the dark room. The anxiety squeezing my throat and twisting my insides eased the moment my eyes landed on him.

He sat in a stiff armchair in the corner of the room, his gaze locked with mine. Lifting the remote, he turned off the television show he'd been watching.

I wondered if I should be alarmed that he'd been watching true crime. Then again, he already knew how to hide a body. Wolves weren't known to be kind when their packs fought, and there was always a body count when the battle was over.

The sudden silence that descended on the room was far too loud.

"You didn't run." My voice shook.

"No. I didn't." His rich, deep voice calmed my anxiety and my pulse slowed. He stood and moved to sit at the foot of the bed. "How are you feeling?"

As the tightness in my chest eased, I was able to draw in a deep breath and let it out slowly. *I'm safe and he's here. Everything is fine.*

"You passed out." Beckett pointed out the obvious.

My cheeks stung, and I forced myself to take another deep breath, trying to stay relaxed and not cave to my rising panic. "I'm okay... I think."

I knew from past experience that I needed to wait a few minutes before I tried to stand, or I'd end up out cold and crumpled on the floor. Glancing at the carpet, I shuddered. A motel room floor wasn't exactly a hygienic place to take a nap.

Relaxing back against the headboard, I narrowed my eyes at him. "You got the handcuffs off, I see."

I was hoping to distract him from asking questions about my little episode in the shower.

"Carrying you and the shower curtain rod while being cuffed was awkward." Beckett leaned forward, picking the cuffs up off the table and spinning them around one of his fingers. "But I can wear them if it makes you more comfortable."

I tried to hide my smile as the mental image of him struggling with a shower rod and my deadweight flashed through my mind. My smile froze when I realized something else.

I was naked.

He'd not only seen, but had also carried my butt-naked body. A hot flush traveled from my head to my toes, and I pulled the blanket up to my chin.

What must he think of me? I'd kidnapped him, aggressively petted the python in his pants, and then all but threw my naked arse into his arms.

At this point, the only thing I hadn't done was unbuckle his pants and plant myself on his lap to enjoy the ride of a lifetime. That mental image caused me to flush again, but this time, the heat surged directly between my thighs.

Abort! Abort! Alarms blared in my skull.

Getting turned on by him was not part of the plan. And Beckett was going to get the wrong idea about what I wanted from him if I didn't get my act together.

I snuck a peek toward the foot of the bed, hoping he hadn't noticed my inner meltdown. A soft glow illuminated Beckett's face as he glanced down at the phone in his lap.

My jaw dropped. No wonder he hadn't run. He'd probably contacted his pack, and they were on the way to the motel now.

"How long?" I asked, voice hoarse.

He glanced up, a single eyebrow raised. "Until?"

"I'm sure you've contacted your pack. How long until they get here?" I rubbed my eyes, trying to stave off the tears of frustration.

Everything was riding on Beckett's willingness to help me, and I'd messed it all up. Why couldn't I have waited until tomorrow to pass out? Oh yeah, because whether I liked it or not, I was dying.

"Take slow breaths, Lilou. I can't have you passing out again." Beckett's deep baritone cut through my panic, and he reached out a hand to squeeze my upper arm in reassurance. "I didn't contact anyone because I was busy searching the internet for directions on taking care of an unconscious kidnapper."

His sexy smirk had my breath hitching all over again.

After I regained control of my breathing, Beckett held up the phone. "What you're doing is admirable."

I found myself staring at an image of my face that had been published along with an article about my promising new research. He was getting close to a truth I didn't want to reveal, a truth I'd kept close to my chest for so long.

Shifting uncomfortably in the bed, I braced for the questions I knew were coming and wondered if I'd even be able to find my voice to give him answers. But to my surprise, Beckett didn't ask me anything.

Instead, he motioned toward the tiny table. "You need to eat."

Standing, he moved to open one of the Styrofoam cups of soup, placing a plastic spoon on the table beside it.

Beckett dropped down into the opposite chair and waited for me to join him at the table.

I glanced down at the beige, scratchy sheet and blanket that covered me, trying to figure out what to do. He might not remember, but I certainly hadn't forgotten that I was wearing nothing but my birthday suit.

There was no way I was going to get up and prance around like I was wearing the emperor's new clothes. Gripping the sheet tighter, I scanned the room, searching for my clothes.

Beckett sighed and stood again. Crossing his arms, he grabbed the hem of his dark tee shirt. When he lifted the shirt up, I could've sworn the world around me began moving in slo-mo, just like a scene from some cheesy movie.

The material slid over his tight, powerful abs and chiseled chest, giving me a show I'd be replaying next time I was having some alone time with my *gun*.

Swallowing hard, I watched him pull the shirt over his head, all the while I was squeezing my thighs together. I knew Beckett was attractive, but how had I missed that he was the living embodiment of a thirst trap?

He looked like he belonged in one of those hot-guys-holding-adorable-animals calendars that raised money for rescues. I'd never wanted to be a small animal, or to be rescued, more.

"Here, slip this on so you can come eat before you pass out again. It's big enough to cover you, so you don't need to feel uncomfortable—even if I've already seen everything."

Beckett muttered the last part quietly, tossing his shirt into my lap.

I glanced at my bag sitting on the floor by the door. My change of clothes was in there, but just the thought of digging it out and dressing fully was exhausting. It had been too long since I'd eaten, so with trembling fingers, I picked up the shirt.

Beckett's earthy scent clung to the fabric that was still warm from his body heat. He smelled like the mountains covered in fog, the first heavy snow of winter, a forest of giant cedar trees and a field glittering with fireflies on a warm summer evening.

It made me think of the comfort of home, but also of adventures and places yet to be explored. Except I knew neither of those things were in my future. Not with Beckett... not with anyone.

Shoving aside the sadness battering at my heart, I pulled the shirt over my head, smiling a little at how it hung off my frame like a dress. To say he was bigger than me would be an understatement.

Beckett settled back into the chair, planting one elbow on the table and popping a bite of food into his mouth. All the while, his gaze never left me. There was an intensity to him, a smoldering hot attitude that made my knees tremble and my pulse flutter.

"Do you need help?" he asked in his low, husky voice.

I was at my quota for stupid things done in a single day. Knowing I needed to put some distance between us if I wanted to prevent myself from going over that limit, I slid to the edge of the bed and touched my feet to the scratchy carpet. I gingerly stood, not quite trusting my legs to carry me. After all, they'd betrayed me when I'd needed them most.

Well, my whole body had betrayed me, but that was nothing new. And things were only going to get worse from here. My health was failing, and there wasn't a magic potion that could reverse the process.

Rising from the bed, I carefully took my first tentative step, wobbling slightly. In a flash, he was by my side, not touching me, but his hands were out and ready to help me if needed.

"I'm okay," I tried to reassure him.

Clearly, he'd heard the lack of confidence in my voice too, because he stayed by my side without saying a word. My body flushed and my heart raced at his proximity. Why was he affecting me this much?

Probably because I hadn't been touched by someone other than a doctor in a long time. Yeah. That was the reason. It wasn't an attraction to Beckett, it was just because I'd been so deprived of interaction that having his full attention on me was wreaking havoc on my whole system.

I was grateful he wasn't asking questions I couldn't—or wouldn't—answer.

He watched me closely as I lowered myself into the chair. There was something guarded in his expression, a new tightness in his features that hadn't been there before, but I didn't understand why.

Beckett moved to sit on the opposite side of the little

round table and picked up a sandwich. "So does that happen often?"

Needing time to think over my response, I opened my soup and inhaled the rich scent as I picked up my spoon. My stomach rumbled in anticipation, reminding me it had been far too long since I'd eaten. Dipping the spoon into the broth, I swirled the carrots, celery, noodles, and chunks of chicken around the container like a snow globe.

"Most of what has happened today has been firsts. My first time kidnapping someone, my first time dumping my food into someone's lap, my first time wearing a guy's shirt." I forced a teasing smile to my lips.

Beckett snorted and gave me *that* look—the one that warned he wasn't in the mood to put up with any shenanigans.

"You know what I meant. How often do you pass out?" he clarified, giving me no wiggle room to back out of the question gracefully.

"I knew what you meant. It's just not something I like talking about," I admitted, then shrugged. "Maybe it's my all-coffee diet. Caffeine crash. Sometimes a girl has to nap, you know?"

His gaze was practically searing my skin. Needing something to do, I lifted a spoonful of soup to my lips. It had long since cooled off, but the taste and texture of the noodles soothed my queasy stomach. When he remained silent, I scooped up a carrot and swallowed another spoonful.

After a long pause, he sighed and polished off the last of

his burger in a single bite. He crumpled the wrapper and tossed it in the small garbage can. Leaning back, he cleared his throat. "So, what's the plan?"

I took another bite, chewing thoughtfully before responding. "I *could* tell you, but…"

"You'd have to kill me," he finished, rolling his eyes.

I laughed and gave him a genuine smile. He didn't owe me anything and he could've left. But he was still here.

At this point, he was here because he wanted to be, not because I was forcing him to stay. Maybe he deserved answers. Besides, what was the harm in telling him the truth? But what if, once his curiosity was satisfied, he wanted to leave?

I'd have to knock him out, cuff him, and force him to stay. It wouldn't be easy, but he was the only person who could help me. I hated that I needed anyone, but some things couldn't be done on my own.

It was a tricky situation. One I still hadn't fully planned out because part of me hadn't believed I'd make it this far, and the other part had been completely delusional and had hoped things would've simply fallen into place for me.

"I'm taking you back to my lab." The words tumbled from my lips before I'd even decided to speak them.

"Are you planning to experiment on me?" he gasped in mock horror, but the sparkle in his eyes told me he wasn't the least bit afraid of me.

"Oh yes. I have a whole notebook full of plans." Leaning into the lie, I wiggled my eyebrows and flipped the spoon over in my mouth, sliding it from my mouth in a suggestive gesture.

His nostrils flared as his gaze dropped to the plastic spoon sliding between my lips and his eyes narrowed.

Butterflies tickled my stomach. I hadn't flirted with anyone since... I didn't even know when. He shifted slightly in his seat before going still.

I smiled. *This is fun.*

CHAPTER 6

Beckett

I tucked my arm around her tiny frame, pulling her tighter against me. After she'd finished eating, we'd spent the next hour getting to know each other.

I'd always thought I was closed off, but Lilou had built walls around herself that were more impenetrable than Fort Knox. Still, she had softened, letting me see flashes of the hurt and pain she kept locked away.

When her eyes had begun to droop and she was yawning every other sentence, I'd helped her get into the bed. Not wanting to make her uncomfortable, I'd laid down on top of the blankets. Lilou had lifted the blankets for me to get under them with a sarcastic comment about making sure to keep my womb-broom in my boxers.

Despite all the space in the bed, my gorgeous kidnapper had scooted against me the moment I'd laid down. There was no denying I was attracted to her gentle nature, her odd sense of humor, and—of course—her sexy body.

I shifted my hips back, not wanting to alarm Lilou with the evidence of exactly how attractive I found her. This was not the time for me to give into lust.

It was more than that, though. The familiar scent from the bathroom had grown stronger until it seemed to be everywhere—the room, the bed, the sheets, her hair, my clothes, my lungs. I could even taste it on my tongue.

I recognized the scent as one I'd thought was impossible to experience ever again.

The scent of my mate.

And it was coming from Lilou.

I took a deep breath, closing my eyes and letting her alluring scent caress my heart and mind.

Mine.

She wasn't a wolf, so how could this be happening?

My wolf whined as another scent touched my senses, this one so faint that it could almost be missed. It was the scent of sickness, and it caused my heart to ache with worry for the woman who'd created so much chaos in my life.

She wasn't well, but I couldn't figure out exactly what was wrong, and she'd withdrawn each time I'd tried to get answers. I wanted to help her, but how could I if she kept hiding the truth from me?

Lilou rolled over, mumbling something in her sleep. I

smiled, remaining still as she cuddled against my bare chest.

Light flashed through the stubborn hotel curtains that refused to close all the way, followed by the loud crunch of gravel. A moment later, a car door opened and closed, letting me know we might have neighbors for the night. I hoped they were the quiet kind... and that their bed didn't squeak.

When Lilou had gone to the bathroom, I'd sent Oliver, my second in command, a message saying I was on a last-minute trip. I'd let him know I hadn't made my meeting and that I needed a favor—for him to take care of the pack until I made it home.

Oliver had texted back almost immediately, letting me know he had it covered, but I owed him. Even through text, I knew he was unhappy. He hated being in charge—a trait he'd had since childhood. But he was a dedicated beta and would take care of the pack, for which I was grateful.

My eyes drifted closed, but Lilou started mumbling again. This time, her noises gave way to actual words.

"The whole cake. I'll eat all of it."

I grinned, burying my face in her wild purple hair. She was irresistible, and the urge to explore her body with my hands and mouth nearly overwhelmed me. But I wasn't about to give in to my intrusive thoughts.

"And then we'll give the yeti a bath," she whispered. "We'll need blow dryers."

I chuckled, trying to stifle the sound so I didn't wake her.

Just as I was drifting off to sleep, I felt her rouse. She scooted away from me and left the bed. Thinking she was going to the bathroom, I bolted upright when I heard the door to the motel room open and close. Where was she going?

Leaping out of bed, I hurried to the door and yanked it open. Lilou looked up at me with wide eyes, her hand poised to knock.

"What on earth are you doing, woman?" I asked, running a hand through my hair.

Lilou bit her bottom lip and her eyes skated away from me. "Well, I thought I was going to the bathroom. Instead, I went out the wrong door and it locked behind me."

"Come back in." I wanted to laugh so badly, but I didn't want to hurt her feelings.

Guiding her inside, I locked the door behind us and watched her make her way toward the bathroom. The girl was a menace, but I found it was one more thing I was beginning to love about her.

"It's a good thing you aren't a heavy sleeper," she mumbled, her voice husky with sleep.

The bathroom door closed behind her, and I settled under the blanket again, throwing an arm over my eyes.

Water splashed in the sink as she washed her hands, then she returned to the bed, sliding between the covers and curling into me.

"You talk in your sleep," I whispered, trying to ignore the way my heart melted and my wolf's tail wagged as she snuggled against me.

"No, I don't," she protested, a smile in her voice.

"Do too." I brushed my fingers down her side, tickling her. "You talked about needing blow dryers because you were giving a yeti a bath. I need to know all about that."

She shook against me, holding back a laugh, but when she spoke, her tone was serious. "It's logical. Have you seen how hairy they are? And imagine how fluffy they'd be if someone took the time to blow dry them?"

Before I could respond, there was a soft click and the glow of the alarm clock and the beam of light sneaking through the curtains from the streetlamp disappeared.

"I think the power's out," I said, stating the obvious.

"When you get top-notch places like this, you have to be prepared for anything. This isn't nearly as bad as the rabbit invasion at the last place." She paused. "Wait, maybe I dreamed that."

I sure hoped so.

"Go to sleep," I mumbled, rolling toward her.

Holding her close, I relished the warmth that spread through me and drifted off to sleep. For the first time in years, I was excited to see what tomorrow would bring.

TEARS STREAMED DOWN *my cheeks as I held my love, my soulmate, in my arms, watching the life leave her eyes. Eyes that shifted between gray and purple.*

I jerked upright, shoving the blankets off me.

Blinking hard, I tried to remember where I was. A motel? Yes, with Lilou.

The bed shifted, and she crawled into my lap, wrapping her arms around me. Her comforting warmth seeped into my bones while her honey and sunshine scent filled my lungs.

"Beckett, it was just a bad dream," she whispered. "You're safe."

It was more than that. I'd not had a dream about the night I'd lost my mate in five years. Thinking of that night still caused me pain, but it had become a dull ache.

But this dream was different, and the pain I was experiencing was sharper than an executioner's sword. Because the mate I'd been holding in the dream was Lilou.

Mine.

Swallowing hard, I buried my hand in her hair and pressed her tight against my chest. A sense of peace calmed my troubled mind, and my breathing began to slow. But it wasn't enough. I wanted more. I wanted her.

I pulled back, and Lilou looked up, her eyes soft and her lips slightly parted. Leaning in, I moved to kiss her, longing to feel her lips on mine. I was desperate for the reassurance that she was here and I hadn't lost her.

Lilou's eyes widened, and she turned her head away.

My terror from the dream shifted immediately into shame.

"I shouldn't have done that. I apologize." Lifting her from my lap, I sat her on the bed beside me, hoping she wouldn't hate me for my poor judgment.

I wanted to tell her what she meant to me, and how much her touch calmed me. That my desire to kiss her wasn't motivated by lust, but rather for comfort. Instead, I said nothing, not wanting her to feel any type of pressure from me.

"No apology needed," she whispered and patted my hand.

"I'll just show myself out," I quipped, hoping humor would dispel any awkwardness filling the space between us.

Her eyes narrowed and I couldn't hold back a chuckle.

"Don't make me cuff you again, mister. I'll do it." She wagged a finger in my direction, then headed toward the bathroom.

"I'd like to use the cuffs on you," I murmured under my breath.

There was no denying I wanted her, but I wasn't about to step out of line again. A cold shower would help to resolve my current predicament, but it was probably out of the question.

She hesitated in the doorway, then turned back toward me. "Um... can I ask for an awkward favor, please?"

"Sure." Awkward was becoming a specialty for me. Besides, I owed her for the failed kiss.

"Can you come in here with me?"

My jaw dropped. "In... the bathroom?"

She nodded. "I never got to finish my shower last night and I'm nervous about showering alone after what happened." An unreadable expression crossed her face, leaving a pink tinge on her pale cheeks. "You probably want to clean up too. We could shower together."

I paused, unsure. If I got in the shower with her, things might get a lot less PG than what she was ready for. "Are you sure that's a good idea? In case you didn't know, I'm attracted to you—"

"It's not like I've never seen a dick before. I work with them most days." She laughed, but I wondered if she meant she literally worked with penises, or if her coworkers were just jerks.

It was smarter to say no, but the memory of what happened during her last shower flashed through my mind and I knew I couldn't. If she got hurt because I was being an honorable prude, I'd never forgive myself. And if I was being honest, the temptation to be near her was hard to resist.

"Okay." I stood, following her into the bathroom.

She lifted my shirt over her head and bent slightly to turn on the water. I looked at the walls and ceiling, trying my best to avoid looking at her naked form. Needing something to do with my hands to keep from grabbing her, I slipped off my boxers, folded them and placed them on the counter by the sink.

Lilou stepped into the shower. Steam billowed over the top of the curtain, still slightly askew from my attempt to fix it last night. Taking a deep breath, I joined her.

Water streamed down her body as she closed her eyes and tilted her head back into the water. It took every ounce of self-control I possessed to keep my gaze on her face, but I managed, my body tense and ready to catch her if she fell.

Without warning, she turned around, her soft backside brushing against an overly sensitive and very rigid part of my anatomy. I sucked in a harsh breath, and for a moment, I worried I might pass out from the sheer pain and pleasure her accidental touch caused.

Lilou shot me a wicked grin over her shoulder, her eyes widening slightly as they trailed down my body.

"I warned you," I said defensively, lifting my shoulders in a shrug.

She didn't say a word, but lifted her face to the water, letting it stream down her face before swiping her hands over her eyes. Steam swirled around us, filling the room.

"Maybe the reason you passed out is because of how hot the water is?" I teased as pink streaks appeared on her shoulders.

"Not likely. I always take hot showers, and I've never passed out in one before." She reached up, adjusting the showerhead so it was aimed at me.

Lilou wrapped her fingers around her wet hair and gently slid down the strands. The hot water stung my skin, but I barely noticed because my eyes were glued to the handful of hair that had come out and lay in her palm. She didn't react, and simply moved the shower curtain a bit so she could drop the wad of hair in the trash.

I was left wondering what could cause her to lose so much hair. Worry overrode my need to give her space, and I stepped closer. Our wet bodies slid against each other, and Lilou shivered.

"Put that thing away, Becks." Her words were playful, but her voice held a husky note that went straight to my cock. She turned to face me, using her arms to cover her breasts. "Or I'll roll up a newspaper and swat you with it."

I burst out laughing, pulling her into my arms. One thing was sure. Life with Lilou would never be boring.

I'd thought the most dangerous thing I'd done in my life was kidnap an alpha wolf.

Boy, was I really freaking wrong.

As it turned out, inviting that alpha wolf into the shower was by far the most dangerous thing I'd done.

It had seemed like the smart decision. I could make sure he didn't escape and he could make sure I didn't pass out. And by showering together, we could get on the road quicker.

That's not the reason you asked him…

My inner voice had a habit of calling me out, and although I wished I could deny it, I couldn't.

I was afraid of falling again, so that part was true. And I did want to hit the road as soon as possible in case his pack was tracking us. But the only reason Beckett was still here was because he wanted to be, not because I was holding him captive.

Admit it. You enjoyed the intimacy of snuggling and didn't want it to end.

I'd known from a young age that I wasn't going to live a normal life, and because of that, I had avoided romantic relationships. One-night stands and casual hookups were safer since they didn't require much in the way of talking, and there were no messy, tangled emotions. Getting my sexual needs taken care of was great, but it left my soul cold and empty.

Last night I hadn't been able to resist the desire to experience what it was like to be held while I slept. I just wanted one night where I could pretend the arms wrapped around me would protect me and love me.

Even though I meant nothing to Beckett, I'd awakened with the glow of happiness warming the hollow sadness I'd grown accustomed to. And I was blaming that for the lapse in judgment when I believed we could shower together without anything happening.

Catching sight of Beckett's erection, and knowing my body had caused it, was a definite ego boost. Especially since my health had begun to deteriorate faster over the past few months. I avoided looking in the mirror, having no desire to see the paleness, or the dark bruises that appeared for no reason, or the way my hair had grown dull and was starting to fall out, or the way my ribs and hipbones had begun to protrude.

Vanity had never been a big deal to me, and I hadn't given much thought to my appearance, but witnessing the outward signs of my worsening condition made it harder to pretend everything was fine. It was intoxicating to know a man as gorgeous as Beckett found me desirable. And when he pulled me into his arms in a playful hug, I couldn't resist the temptation to wrap my arms around his neck and enjoy the intimacy of the moment.

Rivulets of water ran down our skin, causing our bodies to slide against each other. I tried to ignore the way his erection pressed against my stomach, its heat searing my skin and sending a wave of heat straight between my legs.

"Lilou." The single word was low and husky, sending a thrill through me.

"Hm?" I hummed.

Going up on tiptoe, I enjoyed the slide of his length pinned between our bodies under the guise of placing a kiss at the base of his neck.

"We should stop." Despite his words, his hands traveled down my back to rest on my hips. "You feel amazing."

"Do you want me to stop?" I murmured, placing a kiss on his chest.

His fingers gripped my hips tighter. "No, but we're playing with fire. It was hard to resist you in bed with your butt pressed against me, but this is dangerous."

His rough voice and the raw lust vibrating in it gave me the courage to slip my hand between our bodies. My fingers brushed the smooth, rounded tip of his length.

"Oh, yes," Beckett hissed between his teeth, his hips thrusting into my touch.

Taking that as my go ahead, I curled my fingers around his girth and used the water to move up and down his length. Beckett's breathing grew rough, and his body trembled as I found my rhythm.

While my fingers teased and massaged, my lips traveled across his chest. Closing my eyes, I let all my stresses fade away and enjoyed the sensations of his skin pressed against mine, the heat of the water pouring down our bodies, and the fluttering in my belly caused by his hands exploring my body.

His erection grew impossibly hard in my grip, and Beckett wrapped his hand around mine, stopping my movement. "I hate admitting this, but things are going to get messy if you don't stop now."

Opening my eyes, I squinted up at him. Wasn't that the point?

"You don't have to do this. I can take care of things—" Beckett began, but I cut him off.

"Not a chance." Tightening my fingers, I purred.

This was the most thrilling thing I'd ever done... aside from the whole capturing a wolf shifter thing.

Beckett's eyes glowed a brilliant green, and his features seemed to grow sharper. "You're so beautiful."

My body flushed, and I dropped my gaze. His muscles flexed as I continued working his length, bringing him closer and closer to his release. A low growl rumbled in his chest and vibrated through my bones.

"Lilou," he groaned, his body going stiff.

His cock jerked in my hold, spilling the evidence of his arousal over my hand and belly. I slid my thumb over the tip, then licked my glistening fingertip, curious to know what he tasted like.

Beckett growled again, but this time it held a feral edge. "Woman, you have no idea what you are doing to me."

Before I could respond, he grabbed my hips and spun me around so that my back was pressed against his chest.

"I want to touch you." His hand slid lower, sending a thrill of excitement racing through me. "Say yes."

My legs wobbled and his left arm wrapped around my waist, fully supporting my weight. Between the lust clouding my mind, his sexy body holding me as though I weighed nothing, and his lips sucking and kissing my neck, I gave into my desire.

"Yes," I answered, completely breathless. "Touch me."

That was all he needed to hear. Beckett's right hand moved down until he was cupping my sex.

"Oooh." Another wave of slick heat rushed between my thighs.

When his finger traced along my slit, I bit my lip and whimpered. My previous experiences had been dating app hookups, and more of the wham-bam-thank-you-ma'am type of encounters. Nothing about those had prepared me for this type of erotic encounter.

Lust curled tighter and tighter in my belly while my breathing grew ragged. If I wasn't careful, I would end up passing out before he slid a single finger into my heat.

Dropping my head back against his chest, I moaned his name. "Beckett."

His lips moved up my neck, sending electric shocks of pleasure straight to my core. Without warning, his finger delved inside me, causing me to gasp in shock and my eyes to cross.

A second strong finger joined the first, stretching me as he found a rhythm that had me seeing stars. While I struggled to keep myself from passing out, his fingers worked their magic, building the fiery need in my belly to an almost painful level. Unable to help myself, I rocked my hips against his palm.

"Come for me," Beckett rumbled, his lips continuing to kiss and suck along my neck and shoulder.

His fingers moved faster, hitting all the right places, and I fell apart. He held my limp, trembling body as I rode the most powerful waves of pleasure I'd ever experienced.

And even with my senses overwhelmed and my mind clouded with lust, I couldn't help but wonder what it would be like to make love to Beckett if he could make me feel so good with just two fingers.

When my breathing slowed, and the risk of fainting had passed, Beckett turned me in his arms. Holding me to him with an arm around my waist, he grabbed the washcloth, and soaping it up, he began to wash my skin.

Tears pricked my eyes as I discovered, for the first time in my life, what it felt like to be cared for.

AFTER THE SHOWER, we packed up my overnight bag and headed from the dim hotel room out into the bright sun. Climbing into my SUV, we settled in for a long ride.

I spent the next several hours of driving trying not to overthink my rash decision. It had been an idiotic move to allow myself to be distracted while on a literal life-and-death mission.

Parking in front of a fishing cabin I'd rented, I stared at the small wooden structure. It wasn't the fanciest of places, but it had appeared well maintained in the photos, and it was the only place I could find that would let me pay with cash.

The owner hadn't seemed worried about who he was renting to, and I got the impression he was used to renting out to lovers who didn't want to be found out.

Blowing out a long sigh, I rested my forehead against the steering wheel. I'd paid extra to have the cabin stocked with basic groceries, but with my energy waning, I was worried about how I'd have the strength to prepare dinner.

The weight of the world settled on my shoulders and they drooped. Not to mention, I needed to have a conversation with Beckett where I laid out what I needed from him. Closing my eyes, I tried to calm my rising anxiety.

"Are you really taking a nap in your vehicle?" Beckett's voice cut through my tired mind.

I'd been seconds from nodding off, but I wasn't about to tell him that.

"Of course not. Let's go inside." Reaching for the door handle, I stepped out of the car.

He chuckled, opening his car door as well. Not giving me a chance to grab it, Beckett opened the passenger door to get my bag.

"Thank you," I breathed, relieved by his help.

My body was trembling, and I was burning through energy reserves just to stay upright.

His mossy green eyes softened. "No problem."

A warm, fuzzy feeling spread through my belly and I couldn't stop thinking about his hands traveling over my bare skin.

"You are really well behaved for someone who's been kidnapped," I teased, needing to distract myself.

He snorted, amusement dancing in his gaze. "And you are equally terrible at being a kidnapper."

I shook my head. "Touche."

"So, are we going inside?" he asked, turning to take in our surroundings.

It was my turn to snort. "Nope. We drove all this way to just stare at the outside of the cabin."

With heavy feet, I made my way up the tiny roughhewn path that led to the porch. The scent of rain hit my nose and a slight drizzle began to fall.

I didn't hear Beckett walking behind me, but I sensed his presence and knew I wasn't alone. There was an odd comfort in knowing he was with me, which was ridiculous considering the circumstances.

I typed the passcode into the electronic keypad and opened the burgundy painted door. Stepping inside, I was greeted with stale air and a stillness.

Oddly enough, it was the same empty greeting I got when I would leave my lab and head home to sleep and shower. Over the past year, my house had begun to feel as though I were already gone.

Shoving those morose thoughts aside, I dropped my car keys on the table and turned, coming face to face with Beckett.

Like a dance, he crowded me and I stumbled back until my butt bumped into the wall. Beckett planted both hands above my head and leaned in.

I stared up into those intense eyes of his, unable to breathe and hearing my blood pounding in my ears. Heat radiated off him, both comforting and exciting me, as I waited to see what he would do next.

Beckett studied my face with the intensity of a predator, sending a shiver down my spine. Had I misjudged him? Everything I knew about who he was now was second-hand knowledge. We'd parted ways so long ago that he could've changed, and I could be in serious danger.

But my gut wasn't warning me that my life was in danger.

No, it wasn't my body that was in peril. My instincts were warning me it was my heart that was at risk. Beckett could easily break down my protective walls if I let him get too close.

He was someone I feared… because I could love him. And that thought was both exhilarating and terrifying.

I didn't have time for love, though. My destiny was already decided, and that was my work. The research that would live on long after my body was fertilizer. It was that work I'd dedicated my life to and would make all the worry, heartache, and the consequences that were bound to follow my actions in the past two days worth it.

"Now," he growled, "tell me what you want from me."

Warmth rushed south and my stomach quivered. I couldn't breathe, much less tell him what I wanted.

"You didn't risk everything without having a reason. I've been patient, but it's time. I need to know."

He was right, and I'd known this moment was coming. But I didn't know how I was supposed to think with his muscular body pressing me into the wall.

I swallowed hard. "Maybe we should go sit on the couch and talk?"

It was too hard to focus with his hard length poking my stomach and his gorgeous lips so close I could taste them.

"Hm. I think you're stalling." He leaned in closer, so close his breath warmed my neck, sending sparks shooting through me like errant fireworks. "I need to know."

Of course he needed to know. But I was about to ask him for an impossible favor and no matter how I worded it, I knew it was going to sound awful.

I refused to regret any decisions I'd made up to that point. That was the promise I'd made myself at the start of this whole misadventure.

Knowing he'd probably hate me once he got his answer, I leaned in and placed a soft kiss on his lips, wanting to taste him one more time.

He drew in a sharp breath, but kissed me back. The

softness of his kiss was a stark contrast to his hard length that jerked between us. Breaking the kiss, I touched my tingling lips and shoved away my desire to beg him for more. Love and a partner weren't on the table for me.

"Are you trying to distract me, Li?" His breath was ragged, and I longed to kiss him again.

"Partially," I admitted, figuring I might as well be honest.

I was about to make a desperate request, one that only he could grant. Because not only was I running out of time, but he was the only one I would ever ask this of. And by explaining why I'd picked him, I'd also reopen an old wound for both of us.

His eyes narrowed. "Tell me."

My heart banged against my chest hard enough to break ribs. As much as I hated relying on anyone, I didn't have a choice.

I needed his blessing to cancel out my curse.

I needed his protection.

I needed him.

He leaned in closer, his lips grazing my neck. Who was distracting who now?

Part of me wished he'd kiss me until we couldn't fight the desire within us. I wanted to feel complete, if only once. But I also knew that part of me was trying to avoid the discomfort of what was coming next.

Lifting my head, I stared up at the ceiling and tried to bring some semblance of order to my jumbled thoughts.

"There's no easy way to ask this," I whispered around the painful lump in my throat.

He pulled back, but I kept my eyes fixed on the ceiling and avoided his gaze. I couldn't look him in the face while I made my plea.

"Just ask," he growled. "In case it wasn't obvious, there isn't much I would say no to when it comes to you. Do you need money? A place to stay? A bodyguard?"

"I wish." My laugh was brittle, and my eyes burned with tears.

What I needed was a matter of life and death. I finally met his stare, needing him to see my emotions, and that I wasn't joking around.

"Beckett, I need you to bite me."

CHAPTER 8

Beckett

I stumbled back a step as though she'd punched me in the gut.

Of all the things I'd imagined her saying, that hadn't even been in the realm of possibilities. I blinked, trying to wrap my head around the insanity of her request. Hardly trusting my legs to stay under me, I stepped back until I could sag into a chair.

How could she be so heartless as to ask me for this when she knew how much it would hurt?

Lilou moved forward, her eyes shimmering with tears. She reached toward me, but her hand only brushed my arm before she lowered it to her side.

"That's a big ask." I shook my head, not even willing to hear her reasoning. "One I can't agree to."

Her shoulders drooped, and she dropped into a chair across from me.

I watched her, wondering if this was some type of elaborate prank. If it was, it wasn't funny.

"Beckett, you have no idea how much I hate to even ask you for this. But I need your help." Her soft tone soothed some of the raw pain her request had stirred inside me.

"The werewolf gene is considered a blessing to most," she whispered, lowering her head until her forehead rested on her arms on top of the table. Her wavy purple hair fell forward, like a waterfall, and hid her face. "But I'm one of the cursed."

For a second time in less than five minutes, her words hit me like a physical blow. That scent on her... the one I couldn't place. Now I understood why it was so familiar and so alien all at once.

"You have the mutation, don't you?" I asked.

If she did, she was one of the unluckiest people on Earth. The mutation was so rare, I could count on one hand the number of cases that had occurred over the last century.

Wolves didn't get the mutation, but some unlucky humans did if there was a wolf somewhere in their ancestry. My species rarely took humans as a mate, and when they did, they tended not to procreate. This made the odds of inheriting the mutation slim, but it wasn't impossible.

What she was asking was risky—for both of us.

I cleared my throat. "If I bite you and you turn, you'll die." And that was just one of the struggles we'd face if I went along with her plan.

"I know. But I don't plan to shift," she murmured, still not looking at me.

"You're forgetting something." I crossed my arms over my chest. "Biting you will mark you as my mate."

The implications of that alone left me worried she hadn't thought this through. There had never been an alpha with a human mate, so who knew how my pack would react? But being separated after marking her would be cruel to both of us. It would cause me to be distracted, which was a dangerous state of mind when leading a pack.

"I didn't forget. That's the only reason I could ask you— because I knew I wouldn't be taking you from a fated mate who was searching for you." Her words were so soft, I wouldn't have heard them if I'd been human.

Wolves could bite and claim anyone as their mate, but they only had one fated mate. Despite Lilou's desperation to be bitten, she wasn't selfish enough to risk separating fated mates.

That's why she'd kidnapped me... because my fated mate had died.

She lifted her head, offering me what she probably hoped was a reassuring smile. "But don't worry, you won't be stuck with me. I'll be out of your way in the blink of an eye. I just need a little more time on this earth."

"Don't we all?" I asked, rubbing my forehead to ease the beginnings of a migraine.

"I suppose that's true." Lilou shook her head, her lips twisting in a wry smile. "But I don't think you understand what I mean."

Taking a deep breath, she seemed to gather her courage, but I could still smell the fear and pain wafting from her.

Keeping my voice gentle, I tried to encourage her. "I'm listening."

"Please don't think I'm just being greedy. Heck, if it were just for me, I'd never ask this. I've dedicated my life to research and I've made major breakthroughs. Now, my research is finishing the last test and then it can be presented to the world, where it will be used to save so many lives."

My eyebrows rose. "That's amazing, Lilou. You must be so proud."

I'd read about her studies and some of the medical advancements she'd been a part of, but I didn't realize just how incredibly gifted she was.

"It has nothing to do with pride. I need to be the one to present it. Otherwise, I'm afraid a corporation will steal my work, and charge a ridiculous price that people will be forced to pay if they don't want to die. Money was never my goal... saving lives was." A single tear slid down her pale cheek.

My heart ached, and I longed to wipe it away. "I'm sure things will work out."

What was I missing? I still didn't understand what any of this had to do with me biting her. Was she afraid the drug companies were going to put out a hit on her and she wanted protection?

"Not this time." Her voice shook, and she pressed her

fingertips against her eyes. "My body is breaking down too fast. I'm in a race against the clock and I'm losing."

Every drop of blood in my body turned to ice. "What are you saying?" The words came out far harsher than I intended.

Her swirling gray eyes met mine. "I'm going to die before I can complete it."

I sank back in my chair, staring at her in absolute horror, unable to speak a word.

Lilou took my silence as her chance to forge ahead. "Beckett, I've studied the mate bite. I found a case from fifty years ago where a wolf fell in love with a human who was dying of tuberculosis. He bit her and while the bite didn't heal her, it did stabilize her condition and give them a little more time. There are two other cases that are similar, and in both, the females lived a few months longer."

She moved around the table to kneel in front of me, her eyes pleading with me to hear her out. "I know I'm not dying of a human illness, but I think at most, I'd only live a year and then you'd be free of me. It's also possible my condition has already done too much damage and your bite will give me no more than a week or so. But I'm begging you to please consider it."

This decision could be a disaster, not just for me, but for my pack, and for her. The pack was supposed to be my main concern; it was my duty to protect them.

So why was I torn?

It should've been the easiest *no* of my life.

But the word wouldn't come out.

Lilou's lip trembled, and she stared down at her lap.

"Why me?" I already knew, but I wanted to hear the words from her lips.

"If you bite me, I'm not stealing you from your mate." She looked up, her eyes filled with tears.

We'd both lost so much that day. My mate... her best friend.

Strangely, the pain I felt in my chest at that moment wasn't caused by the memory of my mate's death. No, that loss had mostly healed.

Instead, my heart ached for the woman in front of me, one I'd grown to care about more than I wanted to admit.

Her hand touched my knee, causing my wolf to whine and begin pacing in my mind. He was growing attached to Lilou as well, and if I bit her and she died, I would be left frustrated and alone. I'd be forced to live through the nightmare of losing another mate. The muscles in my jaw flexed as I ground my teeth together and remembered the horror of that pain.

"That was the worst night of my life," she whispered. "I remember you holding her."

I remained silent.

"And I remember that he was found dead." Her voice told me she knew what I did... and didn't disagree with my actions. "He deserved it after what he did. What kind of person hits someone and keeps driving?"

"A monster," I answered automatically.

And to kill a monster, I'd become a monster.

That night, I'd held my mate's broken, mangled body in

my arms as she stared up at me, struggling to breathe. There had been so much blood. The scent of it had filled my nose and lungs.

I'd watched her gaze slide from me as the life had left her eyes. Then had come the rage and the hatred. I'd needed to destroy someone.

"The night she died... you were there." I could see her in my mind's eye.

"I was there. Next to her when he hit her..." She trailed off, wincing as if hearing the sound of Idrie being struck down.

Idrie had been pronounced dead at the scene, and after her body had been taken away, we'd sat on the ground for what had felt like hours. Finally, Lilou had stood and led me back to her house.

She'd put me in the shower and had scrubbed the dried blood from my body. I remembered her gaze meeting mine, and the tears flowing down both our faces as we grieved our shared loss.

"I never saw you again after that night," she said, a questioning note in her voice.

"I left town." After what I'd done to the man responsible for murdering my mate, I'd needed to lie low.

The room was growing dim as the sun moved behind the trees, but neither of us moved to turn on the lights.

"I just want to save more lives," Lilou whispered almost to herself. "All I need is your bite. I promise I'll leave you alone after. When I die, you can have my house and car to sell or keep. I don't have much else to offer."

I'd long ago resigned myself to being alone. In the years since Idrie's death, I'd never found anyone. Until a certain purple-haired spitfire had kidnapped me.

She sucked in a deep breath as if to steady her trembling voice. "And when I'm gone, you'll be able to mark someone else. Someone you love."

I smelled her pain... and her fear. She was terrified and desperate for me to say yes. But what she was asking had never been done. How did I make her see that being marked wasn't the solution?

"If I do this, it can't be undone. We'll be drawn to one another, linked until death. It's a craving that'll grow stronger and more painful the longer we're apart." I caught her chin, forcing her to look at me. "And for humans, the pain is excruciating. How can I accept that I would be causing you to suffer?"

"I'm used to living with pain." Her whisper clawed at my heart. "It's been my constant companion for as long as I can remember. I can handle it."

"And what if I can't let you go?" I stared at her, wondering if she'd truly thought this through.

The animal inside me wouldn't let her walk away. She'd belong to me.

Her eyes widened. Clearly, she hadn't considered that I'd want to keep her. But I wasn't about to make a life-altering decision like this without thinking through every possible outcome.

Still, I hoped I could talk some sense into her and figure out another way... because her plan would end in disaster.

"I—" Her throat flexed as she swallowed hard.

Uncrossing my legs, I leaned forward and waited for her answer.

She tried again. "I hadn't thought of that. But even your bite won't fix me for good. I'm going to die. Soon."

Her voice broke, and she dissolved into tears. I hated that I'd added to her distress with my questions. But we had to discuss them.

The world wasn't always black and white. There were often layers of gray to our decisions that were neither good nor bad. It was up to us to make sure we made the best choices for everyone involved.

But I didn't have a clue what I was going to do.

Lowering myself to the floor, I pulled her into my arms and buried my nose in her hair. I breathed in her sweet scent, rocking her gently until her sobs quieted.

CHAPTER 9

Lilou

I f it hadn't been for the loud growl of his stomach, followed up by my stomach making complaints of its own, we might have sat there for hours.

Wiping the last of the tears from my face, I pushed away from him and stood. "It sounds like I better find something for us to eat before your wolf decides to eat me."

"Only if you ask nicely," Beckett laughed, and the low rumble had my heart doing cartwheels.

"No dessert unless you eat everything on your plate!" I retorted, trying to seem confident despite my burning cheeks.

Beckett's eyes sparkled, and he pushed to his feet. "Then what are you waiting for? Let's eat!"

The teasing banter helped to ease some of the awkwardness from the gravity of our conversation. I was thankful for the reprieve, especially since I knew the full weight of the discussion and its implications would hit me again as soon as I stopped moving and laid down to rest.

Because he was going to say no. I'd seen it on his face. Beckett wasn't callous, and I wouldn't hold his decision against him. I'd seen the pain it had caused him to refuse my request. Strange as it was, he cared for me, and not just as someone to have a quickie with.

His gentleness when he soothed me, and the sorrow swimming in his dark green eyes told me that I mattered to him. And that knowledge made my heavy heart a little lighter.

That wouldn't keep my brain from spinning out of control as I tried to come up with a backup plan—a task I knew was futile. If there had been another option, I wouldn't have kidnapped an alpha.

He was my last hope.

My life's work, my legacy, my desire to help people long after I was gone... all of it would vanish without his help.

If that wasn't depressing enough, I hated knowing my request had hurt him. In my head, I'd gone over every possible outcome to my captive alpha plan, most of which had ended in my death at the hands of a wolf, but it had never occurred to me that he might start caring about me.

I knew it would bring up painful memories of Idrie, something I couldn't avoid, but the sadness I'd seen on Beckett's face had been for me.

Swallowing hard, I opened the fridge door and tried to

think of anything other than the unfair situation we were both stuck in.

I took out thick steaks, bacon, and butter, placing them on the counter. Then I searched the cabinets until I found a pot, pan, and cutting board.

Pulling out an onion and several potatoes from the grocery bag on the counter, I grabbed a knife and began cutting the onion.

Beckett moved to stand near me. He studied my tear-streaked face, then looked down at the onion.

A small smile played around the corners of his mouth. "Here. Let me."

I didn't argue and slid the knife and cutting board toward him. Turning down help when I was exhausted would be stupid. And aside from my actions over the past 48 hours, I wasn't an idiot.

Grabbing the cast iron pan, I put it on the stove to heat up. Beckett was quiet, but I could swear I felt his gaze on me. As I added butter to the pan and lowered the heat, Beckett cleared his throat. Taking a deep breath, I braced myself for his rejection.

But he surprised me. "You know, you didn't have to cook for me. We could have just ordered a pizza from the restaurant we passed a few miles before the turnoff for the cabin."

I glanced over my shoulder at him, surprised by the offer. "You mean five pizzas. Remember, I've studied how much wolves eat," I teased. "Besides, it's the least I can do after everything." I waved one hand, gesturing in a way I intended to indicate the mess I'd made of his life.

Thankfully, he didn't patronize me and tell me it was nothing. "Well, I appreciate it."

The warmth and gentleness in his tone caused hope to flare in my chest. Maybe he wasn't dead set against my plan after all. Heck, maybe after thinking about it, he'd say yes.

When he finished cutting the onions, I scraped them off the cutting board and into the buttery pan. My mouth watered as they sizzled and released their delicious aroma into the air.

Beckett had turned his attention to peeling the potatoes. A fleeting sense of contentment settled on me and I smiled.

He hummed a little tune under his breath and I tried to place it. "What song is that?"

"Nothing," he said quickly.

Too quickly.

"Hang on…" I squinted at him. "Are you humming the song about baby sharks?"

"Maybe," he grunted.

Oh, he absolutely was!

"It's a catchy tune." The big bad wolf's skin darkened as he blushed. "Don't you dare judge me."

With herculean effort, I kept from laughing and arranged my face into an emotionless mask. "This is a judgment-free zone," I declared, using the wooden spatula to gesture toward the kitchen, then stirred the onions.

After he finished chopping the potatoes, I dumped them into the pot of boiling water. "Oh! I had something I meant to show you." I smacked my forehead and strode toward the living room.

Beckett followed me, and the moment we were both in the main room, I abruptly turned to face him.

"This room isn't a judgment-free zone. Baby sharks? Really, Becks?" I dissolved into giggles as he scowled and took several steps back until he was standing in the kitchen.

"I'm never leaving this room," he growled in annoyance, even though his eyes sparkled in amusement.

I laughed harder, and eventually, he joined in. For that brief moment, I was able to pretend my life was normal. I wasn't sick or dying. And I could pretend I was simply spending an evening with a handsome man I was attracted to—a man I was finding it far too easy to imagine building a life with.

Except it was just a cruel illusion. But what was the harm in savoring it while it lasted?

He stirred the onions, and I rejoined him in the kitchen.

"I bet you have worse taste in music." He narrowed his eyes in my direction.

I shook my head. "Classical all the way. You can't make fun of opera or orchestra music without looking bad yourself."

He seemed to reconsider. "Fine. Explain the sparkly vampire books in the trunk of your SUV."

I shrugged. "You don't have to worry. I'm team werewolf all the way." Chuckling, I added, "I'm pretty sure my diary even detailed my crush on him. I nearly died of cringe when I reread those entries last year."

"Good. Just remember, werewolves rule and vampires drool." He continued stirring the onions, and I moved to his side and placed the steaks in with the onions and butter.

"But isn't drooling a canine thing?" I bumped his hip with mine.

His arm wrapped around my waist, pulling me against him faster than my brain could process.

"I only drool around you," he purred, his lips brushing my ear. "You know what else wolves do?"

"Wh-what?" I stammered, struggling to think while he was touching me.

He leaned back and smirked at me. "Lick things we think are yummy."

"Beckett!" I yelped.

His tongue slid across his bottom lip. "And you look absolutely delicious."

"Don't you dare!" I warned him.

Pushing free of his hold, I took a slow step back, as though trying not to excite a wild animal.

Beckett's eyes began to glow, and without warning, he lunged for me. I squealed, running around the island and into the living room. He grabbed me from behind, then turned so that he fell onto the couch and pulled me down on top of him.

I squirmed, but with his arm around my waist, all I managed to accomplish was rolling so that my chest was pressed against his. Our eyes locked, and Beckett used his free hand to push my hair over my shoulder.

Knowing what was coming, I squealed again and

wiggled harder. His tongue darted out, sliding playfully up my neck.

"Ahhh!" I gasped... mostly from shock, but also from the electricity that zapped through me.

"Mmm," Beckett hummed, his fingers sinking into my hair and gently angling my head to give him access to my neck.

This time when he licked me, the playfulness was gone. Slowly, his tongue trailed up my neck, teasing my skin and lighting a fire in my belly.

"Ohhh," I whimpered, closing my eyes to enjoy the sensations he was stirring in me.

His chest rumbled with a snarl that was more beast than man, and I went completely still. I'd heard animals make that sound before—on nature documentaries that showed large predators defending their kills and meals.

What in the knick-knack-paddy-whack was wrong with him? I'd only been joking about his wolf eating me, but now I wondered if it was possible for Beckett to lose control of the wolf. If that happened, would I be in danger?

His tongue disappeared as his lips took its place. We lay there, chest to chest, his left arm wrapped around my waist like a steel band, and his right hand still buried in my hair as his mouth kissed and sucked every inch of my neck.

There was a primal possessiveness to the way he held me and I wondered how he could be so rough yet so gentle at the same time. His chest continued to vibrate with snarls and growls, leaving me confused and unsure of what was going on.

I should've been terrified by the shift in his behavior, but instead, it excited me, and I wanted more. I wanted him to rip my clothes off as his mouth explored my entire body.

My greatest desire in life shifted to wishing he would treat me like a human-sized lollipop.

His left hand slid under my shirt to rest on the bare skin of my lower back, and his erection pressed against my stomach. My breathing was coming in ragged pants, and my temperature spiked.

How could he turn me on within a matter of minutes? I'd always enjoyed sex, but never had I felt the desperate need his touch created in me.

Beckett stiffened and drew in a harsh breath. A heartbeat later, our positions had been reversed, and I lay beneath him as his body pressed mine into the couch.

Opening my eyelids, I stared into his glowing green orbs.

"Lilou." His voice was rough, as though his vocal cords had been damaged.

I said nothing and waited to see what he would do. Thankfully, I didn't have to wait long. Gripping the bottom of my shirt, he pushed it up, baring my stomach and bra-clad breasts to his hungry gaze.

Goosebumps rushed over my skin as the heat of his mouth touched my stomach. Instead of taking his time, his mouth moved quickly up my body. When his tongue flicked out across the swell of skin above my bra, I sucked in a breath.

My breasts ached, begging for his attention, but just as

his fingers moved aside the fabric and exposed my breast, the smoke alarm went off.

"The food!" I shouted.

Adrenaline shot through me, and I shoved him off me with so much force he toppled to the floor. I caught only a glimpse of his befuddled expression as I dashed into the kitchen to move the pot and pans off the stovetop.

Using the spatula, I inspected the food. To my relief, other than a few crispy onions and a few potatoes sticking to the bottom of the pot, our dinner wasn't completely ruined.

The steaks were leaning toward medium-well, rather than my preferred medium-rare, but that was a small price to pay for the pleasure I'd experienced from Beckett's attention.

By the time I finished mashing the potatoes with cream and butter, my breathing had returned to a normal rhythm. Taking two plates from the cabinet, I served up the steaks.

Beckett appeared in the kitchen, watching as I spooned some of the steak butter and onions over the mashed potatoes. With a shy smile, I offered him the plate, which he took with a nod of his head.

I grabbed my plate, along with two knives and forks, and joined him at the table.

Beckett dug into his food while I picked at mine.

"You're moving the food around, but you aren't eating," he pointed out.

"I'm not very hungry." As my body had begun caving to

the effects of the mutation, my appetite had vanished, and even eating small amounts could make me nauseous.

"Li, you need to eat. Maybe that's why you passed out." Beckett cut a small bite from his steak, then held his fork an inch from my lips.

"Eat your food. I heard your stomach earlier," I teased, not liking the way his sharp gaze studied me.

Instead of eating the bite himself, he started moving the fork in circles and loops.

"What the fork are you doing?" I asked, my eyebrows drawing together in confusion as he brought the piece of steak toward my mouth again. "Are you... Are you doing the airplane?"

"Yes. Now, open up." He waited for me to obey his order, and when I did, he fed me the bite.

His gaze heated as he continued to stare at my mouth, and heat flooded my belly in response.

Whether I wanted to or not, I was falling for him.

Pulling his eyes away from me, he took a bite of the steak. Then he picked up a bit of potato, making buzzing sounds as he moved the fork toward my face again.

It was breathtakingly sweet that he cared enough to make sure I was eating, especially since my studies had taught me that wolves didn't share their food with anyone outside their pack.

But the absurdity of the intimidating alpha wolf feeding me was too much, and I burst out laughing. Beckett's mouth twitched, but he lifted an eyebrow and waited for me to take the bite.

Pulling myself together, I took the potatoes from his fork and basked in the glow of his attention. No matter what happened in the future, this moment was mine to keep forever.

We finished eating and washed the dishes together. Then came the matter of where we would sleep. Beckett offered to sleep on the couch, but taking his hand, I led him to the bedroom.

"Just snuggles; no getting handsy," I warned as we climbed beneath the covers.

As we lay there in the dark, him holding me as the little spoon, I whispered the question that weighed on my mind. "What if I find a way to give you something you want in return for your bite?"

His arm tightened around my waist. "It's not about me getting something in return. Your desire to save lives is the most convincing cause I could imagine. But the cost is high."

"I know, but like I said, you'll only be bound to me for a short while."

His chest rumbled with a sound of frustration. "There's more to it than that, Lilou."

Tears burned in my eyes. "I don't understand."

"There's a... closely guarded secret we wolves keep about marking our mates." He released a pained sigh. "I'm not at liberty to share the secret with anyone outside the pack. If you were a wolf, I could share, but you're not. Wolves know what they're getting into, but humans don't. A few wolves take human mates, but they are outcasts because of it."

"So you can't tell me the secret because I'm not in the club, but you can't bring me into the club without telling me?" I wasn't even surprised that life continued to throw me unfair curveballs, but that wasn't what had my heart growing heavier.

Why hadn't I realized what I would be asking Beckett to risk for me? I'd mistakenly believed we could keep the bite a secret. After all, it wasn't like I'd be around long enough for him to bother introducing me to people. But by biting a human, I was asking him to risk losing the respect of his pack—his family. That would be a lot to ask of a man who loved me, let alone one I'd kidnapped.

Squeezing my eyes shut, I tried to keep the tears at bay and prayed that sleep would come quickly.

CHAPTER 10

Beckett

I woke before the sun rose, and like an absolute creep, I watched Lilou sleep. The dark wasn't an issue for me thanks to my wolf DNA, and I was able to count each of her long eyelashes that rested against her cheek.

She tried to appear strong, but I could see past the mask she hid behind. Underneath, she was incredibly fragile. This was only the third day I'd spent with her, but I could see the changes. Her skin was so pale that it was almost translucent in the fading moonlight.

Worst of all was the way her temperature had been steadily dropping, her body struggling to find the energy to keep her warm. As though sensing my thoughts, she scooted closer to me, burying her face against my chest and snuggling into my heat.

Wrapping my arm around her, I held her close and rested my chin on the top of her head. I wanted to hold her like this every day for the rest of our lives, but that would come too soon. Life was cruel.

I hated the position I now found myself in. And I hated having a secret that Lilou needed to know, but I couldn't tell her.

Every second I spent with her made the longing to stay grow stronger. I needed to find the strength to leave, because the line between what was a good idea or a bad idea became increasingly blurry the longer I was with her.

Lilou was fun, adorable, and the overwhelming urge to protect her had my wolf running laps inside me. She was everything I'd ever wanted.

Fate had given me Idrie as my mate, and while she'd been a wonderful woman, I hadn't chosen her for myself. If it hadn't been for our wolves pushing us together, I doubted either of us would have picked each other as mates. Friends, yes. Partners, no. But the bond had drawn us together, and we'd begun to accept each other.

Things were different with Lilou. It wasn't just my wolf that wanted her... I wanted her to be mine. She was every-thing I'd ever hoped to have in my partner.

Closing my eyes, I breathed in her sweet scent. My stomach pitched as I caught the sour note of the mutation intertwined with the scent of death that was growing stronger as her body continued to shut down.

Maybe marking her wasn't such a bad idea after all. She was the one begging for my bite, so surely she'd forgive me when she learned the truth I was keeping from her.

No. I couldn't give in to the urge to mark her. It would only end in heartbreak for both of us. I couldn't protect her from her illness. My mark might buy her time, but was it worth the pain it would cause for both of us?

For the next two hours, I held her, trying to convince myself to leave once she awakened. Eventually, her breathing changed, and she pressed a soft kiss to the skin just over my heart.

"If I guess the secret, will you tell me?" Lilou whispered, arching her back as she stretched.

I gave her a small smile. "That's not how secrets work."

She rolled her eyes. "Fine. Just so you know, secret or not, I'm still willing to be bitten. It's still worth it to me."

I sighed and shifted to a sitting position. "I'm going to take a shower."

Maybe that would wake me up and help me find some clarity.

Closing the bathroom door behind me, I undressed and took in the clean lines of the room. The walls were stark white, with a touch of gray along the baseboards. I turned the faucet until the water was hot enough to turn my skin an angry red.

As I stepped under the slippery needles of water, the scorching heat rinsed away some of my stress and washed it down the drain. Relief seeped in, but I knew it would be short-lived.

I needed to talk to Lilou about my decision, and then I

needed to get back to my pack. Oliver was no doubt doing a good job, but a beta couldn't run a pack for long. He probably wanted me back sooner rather than later. Not to mention, I missed my pack. Wolves weren't meant to be away from their family.

Dumping some shampoo into my hand, I scrubbed my hair. There wasn't a satisfactory answer to this situation.

As much as I wanted to claim her as mine, I couldn't bite her. But I also didn't want to leave her. At the end of the day, I would have to live with whatever decision I made.

If I bit her, both our worlds would change. And probably not for the better.

An alpha mating with a human, even just for show, wouldn't be well received by most wolves. Humans were weak and she wouldn't be able to bear pups or carry on the alpha bloodline. I wouldn't care if it meant I could have her as my mate, but it could cause my pack to crumble. Even if I explained that the arrangement with Lilou was temporary, none of them would listen or care.

Perhaps I could explain this would improve human and wolf relations. Humans knew wolves existed, but they saw us as beasts of the shadows.

If I framed this as a PR move to shift how humans see us, it could open opportunities for wolves to be accepted more in human society. But I couldn't stomach using her, even if I was simply using it as an excuse to keep my pack calm about the decision to bring in a human.

This is the first time in a long time I'd faced a situation that had no good outcome. Because if I didn't mark her, she would die before her work was complete. And I'd have to take some personal responsibility for the lives lost due to my inaction.

So what was the lesser of the two evils?

I planted my hands on the shower wall and let the hot water course down my face. If I was honest with myself, I'd admit that I wanted her, regardless of the repercussions. And I didn't just want her in my bed. I wanted her in my life.

Turning the water off, I stepped out of the shower and grabbed a towel.

I dried quickly and dressed in the spare set of clothes we'd stopped and bought on the way to the fishing cabin. I stepped from the bathroom, steam billowing out behind me.

The house was quiet, and I tiptoed toward the living room. I stopped in place when I caught sight of her curled up on the couch. Had getting up exhausted her so much that she'd already fallen back asleep?

Her body was motionless, and I listened for her heartbeat, needing to reassure myself she was okay.

With soft steps, I knelt by her side. She was wrapped up in a knitted blanket in hues of white, gray, and black. I wanted to scoop her up into my arms and carry her back to bed. She deserved to be fed breakfast in bed and then cuddled while she napped.

My chest ached with the knowledge that I couldn't be the one to love her. I couldn't stay.

Pain and loss seeped through me as I stared at Lilou's

beautiful face. My soul reached out for her. I'd been alone for so many years that I'd almost grown accustomed to it. But the happiness I'd experienced the past three days had shown me how empty and cold my life truly was.

Years ago, I'd been filled with hope that I would build a wonderful life with Idrie. But before that could happen, I'd been condemned to a life of loneliness because of one careless man.

I knew in my heart that Lilou was my second chance at happiness. If I marked her, I'd feel complete. But only until she left this world, and I was plunged back into darkness.

Biting her would ease my short-term suffering, but it would add so much grief to my life. The only thing worse than losing one mate... was losing *two*.

When wolves lost their mates, they lost themselves—just as I'd lost myself for a while after Idrie's death, and I hadn't even marked her. I'd been focused long enough to go after the man who had killed her, but then I'd gone absolutely feral.

It was nothing short of a miracle that I'd found my way back to society. The world had eventually shifted back into focus, like kaleidoscope pieces falling into a familiar pattern.

I'd returned to the pack to lead my people... alone.

If I lost myself again and didn't find my way back, my pack would have to put me down. It was the humane thing to do. I doubted I would survive that maddening pain again.

CHAPTER 11

Lilou

I opened my eyes and blinked. The fog of sleep cleared from my mind like clouds parting to allow the sunshine through. My eyes landed on the chair across from me.

Beckett had one arm thrown over his eyes, and his chest rose and fell in steady breaths. I couldn't help but admire him, loving the way he was sprawled out, looking relaxed... and delicious. The man was a thirst trap, and I was embarrassingly desperate.

Moving slowly, I sat upright, giving my body time to adjust. I touched my feet to the chilly hardwood floor and winced at the cold jolt that shot up my legs and through my body. With careful, measured movements, I shifted my weight onto my feet and stood upright.

I braced for a wave of nausea or faintness. And because I was lucky, I got both that morning. My stomach twisted and bile threatened to choke me, all while my body trembled and the cold sweats started. As black crowded the edges of my vision, I sagged back down on the couch for a moment, waiting for one or the other to fade.

A shower would have been a wonderful way to start the day, but falling first thing in the morning did not. Given that hot water raised my blood pressure and made me more likely to kiss the porcelain tub, I decided to skip it.

As my vision returned to normal, I slowly stood again. Beckett hadn't eaten enough the past two days, and that was my fault. I decided to fix that. It was the least I could do after putting him in such a messed-up situation.

Heading to the bedroom, I changed into comfy sweats and a tee-shirt. I breathed a sigh of relief to be in clean, soft clothes. I picked up my brush and gently ran it through my hair, trying not to notice how much was collecting in the bristles. When I finished getting out the tangles, I twisted my hair up into a bun on top of my head.

I tiptoed through the living room, not wanting to wake Beckett. Creeping into the kitchen, I gathered everything I needed to make him a breakfast he wouldn't forget. By the time he woke up, there would be a platter full of food waiting for him.

Peeking into the living room, I checked to make sure he was still sleeping and found that he hadn't moved. Wolves generally had a lot of energy, so his fatigue was likely a result of not consuming enough calories. What kind of horrible human being was I that I would practically starve a wolf?

Breathing a sigh of relief, I bent down to grab three cast iron pans from a bottom cabinet. One for bacon and sausage, one for eggs, and one for pancakes.

I waltzed around the kitchen, gathering ingredients and bowls for mixing. As I turned around to get to the fridge and get eggs, my forehead came in contact with a wooden cabinet door I'd left open while searching for bowls.

The thud echoed through the room as pain burst through my head. "Son of a bibliography!"

I paused, rubbing the aching spot and trying not to laugh at myself for being such a dummy.

Glancing into the living room, I watched Beckett's chest rise and fall a few times. Clearly, he was a sound sleeper. Closing the cabinet door, I turned toward the fridge.

I didn't know what was wrong with me, but I could swear I was more accident prone around him. Or maybe I was just distracted by something... like his gorgeous green eyes or sexy body.

Shaking my head, I pushed all thoughts of Beckett from my mind and got the bacon frying. When that task was completed, I turned my attention to making the pancakes. Adding in a touch of cinnamon and vanilla, I mixed the batter.

Only when the batter was smooth and ready to use did I turn back around. And that was when I saw the smoke rising from the pan of sizzling bacon.

Oh, great! I was going to set off the fire alarm. Again.

I rushed toward the pan, but before I could remove it from the heat, flames erupted in the pan and I let out a squeak of shock and stepped back. This had never happened before, and I didn't know what to do. But I knew I needed to figure something out before I burned the house down.

From the corner of my vision, I caught movement as Beckett strode into the room. Instead of looking panicked or angry, he appeared totally at ease. He walked right up to the flaming pan, picked up a metal lid I'd set aside, and covered the fire. With the fire tamed, he turned down the heat.

"I, uh... thank you. I swear I'm a good cook."

He arched an eyebrow at me and a playful defensiveness washed over me. "It's not my fault! You've got me all distracted."

His eyebrows shot up and he chuckled. "You're blaming this on *me*?"

I hadn't planned to, but it was too late to backtrack; I was committed. With a nod of my head, I grabbed the mixing bowl filled and ladled some of the pancake batter into a pan, still feeling his stare on me.

"And I suppose I'm also the reason there's a red mark on your forehead?" Beneath his amusement, I thought I caught a hint of concern.

His reaction highlighted the reason I didn't want anyone in my life as my health declined. I didn't want people to pity or worry over me.

Blushing, I reached up and touched the spot again. "I walked into a cabinet. I think my last three brain cells are on vacation."

He moved closer to me, his eyes shifting back and forth between my eyes and my lips. As his hand cupped my cheek, I felt myself leaning into him. There was a click as he shut off the gas stove. I guess he was anti-burning the house down, which was good, since I'd woken up as an aspiring arsonist.

With no further warning, he lowered his lips to mine. His kiss was a study in contrasts. Gentle, yet hungry. Soft, yet powerful.

As his tongue traced along the seam of my lips, I gave him access to my mouth, allowing him to deepen the kiss. My body melted against him, and his arms wrapped around my waist as he supported my weight.

Far too quickly, he leaned back. His breath fanned across my skin as he gently touched his lips to the tender spot on my forehead in a way that left me ready to melt into a puddle at his feet.

I desperately wanted him to be mine, even if only for a matter of days... or weeks.

"What if I promise never to tell?" I whispered, still cradled in his arms. "I'm not going to live long and I swear I won't be a pain."

His body stiffened up, and I was sure he was mad at me for begging. I'd ruined a sweet moment with my comment because I couldn't keep my mouth from rambling.

Still, I didn't understand why he couldn't—or wouldn't—help me. What secret would be so impossible for humans to wrap their heads around that wolves had kept it to themselves for centuries?

CHAPTER 12

Beckett

"I'm not going to live long and I swear I won't be a pain."

Her words were like a knife through my heart. She thought that was a reassurance, but in truth, it was the worst thing she could have said. I was falling for her, and deep down, I believed I had the strength to walk away from my pack if they rejected her. Having this ray of sunshine and exuberant joy as my mate, to love as mine, would be worth whatever I faced.

But that life of happiness with my mate couldn't be mine… because she was going to die.

I'd walk away from my pack, only to be plunged into the abyss of dark loneliness when she passed from this world.

Lilou went up on tiptoe, placing soft kisses along my jaw and murmuring apologies that barely registered. What had started as an amusing side quest had ended up giving me a taste of the life I craved... a life I couldn't have.

My frustration, rage, and lust wove together, a bomb ready to go off. I struggled to contain the emotions battering me, but it was a lost cause. Because when her lips brushed against mine, she set fire to that short fuse.

Touching and snuggling Lilou over the past few days had been a special kind of torturous bliss. It had been far too long since I released the pent-up need, and I could no longer hold back the raw desire I felt for the beautiful little female molding her body against mine.

The beast inside me lifted his head as hunger overtook me. With quick movements, I roughly backed her up until she was pressed against the wall.

"I want you," I growled and used my knee to part her thighs. "My wolf wants you."

She blinked up at me in stunned surprise, her perfect lips forming an O.

"If you don't want me to touch you, you need to go to the bathroom and lock yourself in. Turn on the fan to help cover your scent." I gritted out the warning, feeling my eyes flicker between those of my wolf and those of my human form.

"N-No," Lilou whispered. "This is where I want to be."

Brave words for a human who was facing down a predator. Still, I caught the spike in her heart rate and the sweet-and-spicy scent of her fear mixing with arousal.

I breathed in, enjoying the taste of it on my tongue and coating my mouth. It was intoxicating, and affected my wolf in much the same way kerosene affected an out-of-control fire.

Grabbing her hips, I brought them forward until she was balanced on my thigh, and her pliant body pressed to mine like a puzzle piece. My mouth found hers in a demanding kiss, and Lilou parted her lips, giving in to me without hesitation.

Even lost in my lust, I took in a deep breath to check her emotions, needing to know she wanted this, too. Her desire and excitement filled my lungs, assuring me she wasn't regretting her decision to stay rather than run.

I gripped her hips, rocking her forward. She gasped into my mouth and her entire body trembled.

"Does that feel good?" My voice was harsh, and I hoped it wouldn't scare her.

"Yes. Oh goodness, yes," she breathed, her pale skin flushing to the point she appeared almost healthy.

I slid her against my thigh a second time, encouraging her to take what she needed.

"Then show me," I demanded, wanting to see her give in to the hunger I saw mirrored in her eyes.

She responded eagerly. Looping her arms around my neck to give her better control, her hips shifted against my leg. Her motions started slowly, but quickly grew sharp and uncontrolled. There was a desperation in the way she moved that told me she was just as deprived as I was of touch.

Her alluring scent wrapped itself around us, and the quick beat of her heart thundered in my ears. It was too much, and I moved a hand to the back of her head, angling her mouth so I could deepen our kiss.

Lilou moaned as her tongue danced with mine and I hungrily swallowed the sound. Finding her rhythm, she continued riding my leg. My thoughts scattered, my stresses vanished and all that mattered was this perfect moment with Lilou—the woman I wanted as my mate, regardless of the obstacles that stood in our way.

Leaning back, I looked into her eyes as her movements became more frantic.

"I want you more than anything," she whispered.

My heart leaped, and my wolf surged forward, eager to claim her. I wanted her too, but for now, I'd have to settle for this. If we pushed this physical encounter further, I knew I'd wind up marking her regardless of the reasons I shouldn't.

"But I can't fall in love right now. I can't get distracted," she rasped between breaths as she clung to me.

I barked a dark laugh. "Your dirty talk needs work."

Her gray eyes swirled with lilac, triggering a memory of being in her house after the accident. She'd had a basket of lilac blossoms in the bathroom, and their fragrance had helped mask the sharp metallic odor of blood and death that had clung to me. I'd noticed that their color matched her eyes. It was weird the things that your brain latched onto when going into shock.

"I'm here. You're not alone," she'd whispered that night,

pushing me into the shower, clothes and all, turning on the hot water.

As humanity slipped from my grasp, the rest of the world had gone blurry. But not Lilou. She'd been the one thing in sharp focus, and I'd followed her as she stepped into the shower, fully clothed, and kneeled beside me.

I'd sat on the floor of the shower, watching my mate's blood turn the water red before swirling around the drain and feeling my bloodlust growing. She'd alternated between recalling her treasured memories with Idrie, and reminding me I was strong and I had a pack that needed me.

I had clung to her words, knowing it was the last fragile thread keeping me from being sucked into the yawning abyss that called to my beast. Maybe if I'd leaned on her during my grief, things would have turned out differently.

Still, I'd seized the opportunity to escape through the bathroom window when she'd left the room to answer the front door. I'd focused on my desire for revenge and the world had gone blurry as my sanity slipped.

But I knew without a doubt that Lilou was the only reason I'd retained that tiny part of myself that had allowed me to find my way back.

Maybe I'd come back because I'd unconsciously remembered she was out there. That I wasn't alone.

Now she needed me, but I was paralyzed between bad decisions that all had heartbreaking outcomes.

I knew one thing for sure. This time, I wasn't going to

leave her alone in her grief. I'd find a way to be there for her.

"I'm sorry," she murmured, pulling me from my inner musings. "I wasn't trying to ruin the moment."

Her fingers brushed along my jaw, and her warm touch calmed the turmoil inside me. She hadn't ruined anything, but I wasn't ready to share my thoughts or concerns about the powerful effect she had on me.

The mixture of vulnerability and desire on her face had my cock throbbing painfully, and every ounce of my self-control shifted to not stripping her down and taking whatever she was willing to give me.

My vision blurred, but she remained in focus. The only thing that mattered to me at that moment. I loved the way her heat seared my leg as she rode me, and gripping her hips again, I ground her against me.

"Lilou, I can't get enough of you." I touched my lips to hers, then buried my face in the crook of her neck and inhaled her sweet scent. "I love your smell."

She giggled.

I pulled back and scowled. "Was that funny?"

She shook her head. "It's just... I felt like such a weirdo for sniffing your hair when I kidnapped you, so now I don't feel so bad. But you smell so good."

"So do you." I trailed my tongue along her velvety soft neck, loving her unique, delicious flavor. "I love the way you taste."

She trembled, her breathing turning to soft whimpers that told me how close she was to coming apart.

"I love the way you respond to my touch." Unable to resist my wolf's urging, I opened my jaw and gently pressed my teeth to her neck.

Taking my time, I slowly dragged them along her skin. She shivered and sucked in air, struggling to catch her breath. I would've been worried if I'd caught even a hint of panic coming from her, but I could only taste desire and hunger.

"I want you." Moving one hand from her hips, I cupped her breast, enjoying the way her eyelids fluttered. "I need you."

Her whole body tightened and shuddered. She leaned her head back against the wall in a way that had me longing to bite her so she would wear my mark.

"Beckett!" My name came out strangled, as though someone was wringing the word out of her.

She struggled to catch her breath, and I could feel her body tightening and relaxing even though she was only riding my leg. My whole being shouted for me to undress her and bury myself inside her. I'd never been so painfully hard or this desperate for release.

But the part of my brain that was still working knew if I made that move, I would end up marking her. I wouldn't be able to stop myself. Hades! My control was already hanging by a frayed thread.

She clung to me, shivering as her body finally went still. Moisture danced in the air around us and I inhaled it like a man starved, wishing I could taste her.

I doubted she'd try to stop me if I carried her to the

bedroom, removed her pants, and kneeled between her legs to bury my tongue in her silky heat. But I had to stop before I lost all control.

With careful hands, I released her, making sure she was steady on her feet. She braced herself against the wall, staring at me in stunned surprise as I backed away from her.

Sensing she was a bit dazed, I guessed nobody had ever had her ride their leg to orgasm. My wolf pranced around proudly at the knowledge she wasn't used to sexual experiences like the one she'd just had.

Which made me wonder...

If she was this stunned after what we'd just done, how would she react if I took her to bed and made her mine?

Realizing my thoughts had taken a dangerous turn, I retreated down the hall to the bathroom. I closed the door behind me and sat down heavily on the edge of the tub. Burying my face in my palms, I tried to will away the desire eating at me.

The sexual desire I could deal with, but it was the desire to claim her that felt as though it were shredding my soul.

She couldn't be mine, and it was killing me.

CHAPTER 13

Lilou

I peeked over at Beckett from my spot on the couch.

Four hours had passed since... well, since he'd cornered me, pinned me to a wall, and had me hump him like a horny teenager. I couldn't stop thinking about the tender words he'd spoken in his sinfully husky voice, or the feeling of him overpowering me while staying so gentle. It was erotic, yet romantic, and my body was tangled up in knots over it.

As though sensing my stare, he lifted his head and his gaze locked on me. I froze like a cornered animal that had been caught. Beckett arched a single eyebrow, confirming without words that he knew I was staring at him.

After he'd disappeared into the bathroom, I'd needed to sit and rest. My energy levels were barely enough to keep me upright, and I'd burned through an entire day's worth making out with the sexy wolf.

I was running out of time, yet I was still on the couch, resting. There were so many things I needed to get done, and I knew I shouldn't have allowed myself to get distracted.

But why shouldn't I get to enjoy at least a little of the limited time I had left? The battle between my head and heart went around in endless circles, like boxers in a ring.

I shouldn't be so selfish, but I shouldn't refuse myself a few simple pleasures.

I shouldn't be wasting time, but I shouldn't push myself when I'm too tired to function.

My body was exhausted and longed for rest. But I was going to experience the ultimate rest very soon, and none of what I'd done would matter if I didn't get things wrapped up before my endless dirt nap.

I knew there were at least two competing companies gunning for my research. If they got their hands on my work, they'd steal everything and charge ridiculous prices for the lifesaving intervention.

It had been proven time and again that people would pay whatever it cost to save their lives and the lives of their loved ones, even if it condemned them to be in debt forever.

I needed to finish the research and make sure I put it out into the world before I died. Nearly every penny I'd made in research, I'd invested into my work. I'd also spent the majority of my off time convincing big-hearted donors to help fund the research. This meant it was my research to do with as I pleased.

But if I died before I could show my research to the world, the lab that had offered me a workspace in exchange for being listed as a contributor on my research papers might try to lay claim to my research.

The stress had probably added to the damage being done to my body, but there was nothing I could do about that. I just had to hang in there a bit longer.

Beckett stood and made his way to me. I narrowed my eyes as he approached, then circled me.

"What are you up to... Ooooh!" I moaned as he placed his hands on my shoulders and his thumbs pressed into my aching muscles.

He chuckled, but his thumbs continued to work the tight knots in my shoulders and down my spine.

"You're awfully tense," he said, his tone implying that he'd expected me to be relaxed.

Probably because he's used to women being puddles of lovesick goo after he rocked their worlds...

"Yeah. I'm sitting here because I'm exhausted, but I'm stressed because I'm not accomplishing anything," I sighed. "It's an endless, vicious cycle that seems to drive my entire existence at this point."

His magic hands continued to work my muscles, seeming to know exactly where to rub and press to ease the tension.

Closing my eyes, I enjoyed the massage, trying my best

not to think about how it would feel for his fingers to move… down there.

Would he touch me with as much skill as he'd shown already? I mean, what we'd done had been a first for me, but he seemed so nonplussed about everything. Maybe he had so much experience it was simply sex for him at this point, and nothing to get too excited about.

As the tension melted from my body, I rolled my shoulders, feeling looser and more relaxed. With every motion of his fingers, heat rippled through me, building like molten lava deep in my core.

He somehow managed to make me hot, excited, and confused all at the same time. I'd be absolutely annoyed if I wasn't so intrigued. It was unfair that I was a grown woman, yet he made me feel like an inexperienced teenager.

"Lean forward," Beckett ordered, moving his hands down my spine when I obeyed.

Just as he got to the band of my sweats, he stopped. Every ounce of self-control I had was funneled into not groaning out loud from disappointment. But before I'd even closed my mouth, he scooped me up and laid me down on the couch.

Face down, I felt him straddle my backside, and I shifted my hips from side to side, hoping he was about to do what I hoped he would. There were far too many layers of clothing between us, but maybe he was planning to take his time.

He lifted my shirt and excitement flooded my veins. Was this really about to happen?

His thumbs pressed into the flesh on either side of my spine and he pushed them up my back. Then he started at the bottom, repeating the same steady motions.

It was incredible—not as incredible as I imagined sex with him would be—but pretty freaking amazing, nonetheless.

His weight disappeared, and I turned to face the TV, catching sight of my reflection in the black screen.

Oh, my goodness, I mouth at myself. I would do anything he asked of me right then. *Anything*.

My desire to be bitten had grown, but less because of the extra time and more because I longed for him to bind us together. Having Beckett tied to me and part of my life excited me in a way I'd never experienced.

Probably because I'd never thought I could have a partner... or be loved.

A twinge of guilt twisted my stomach at the thought of Idrie. Beckett had belonged to her, so maybe I didn't have any right to desire him.

But was there any harm in us finding each other a decade later? Besides, I didn't want to take her place or replace his memories of her. My heart just wished he could have a small spot for me.

He strode back into the room, oil in hand.

"Where did you get that?" I asked, my eyebrows shooting up.

Beckett smirked at me. "I noticed it earlier in the basket of complimentary toiletries."

Once more, he straddled my hips, and I tried to ignore

the electric excitement lighting up every nerve ending at the contact of his length pressed against my butt. Even through the fabric separating us, I could feel his heat. With no small amount of effort, I remained still, but all he had to do was say the word and I would happily be his hot dog bun.

His rough hands rubbing together sent a shiver up my spine before he even touched me, and the mint-scented oil caused my nose to tingle.

"How do you handle strong scents like that?" I asked, curious. "Wolves have a keener sense of smell than the average person."

"We get used to them." He sounded unconcerned as his hands slid up my back, causing a string of popping sounds to follow in their wake.

"This is amazing," I moaned, my brain clouding with absolute bliss. "Marry me."

He froze.

I blinked, trying to remember what I'd said... then groaned. "Ugh! That was supposed to be a joke. I didn't mean it! Well, I didn't not mean it, but you know what I meant—or didn't mean."

Closing my mouth, I stopped the flood of increasingly humiliating words. His hands began to move again, and I exhaled in relief.

I hated that he probably felt like I was pressuring him to bite me. But on the flip side, I felt equally bad thinking of the lives that could be lost if I wasn't able to complete my life's work.

The utter exhaustion of my body wasn't easing up—it

was worsening. And it was looking more and more like I'd be unable to finish my work.

"You don't know what you're asking." His voice was husky, as though he were torn up over the situation as well.

"I know. And I'm sorry I've pulled you into my mess." My voice trembled. "I wish you could tell me why, but I understand pack loyalty."

"As a leader, if I don't follow the rules, how can I expect my pack to?" He made a valid point.

"Who would ever know? I wouldn't tell." I mean, it was literally a victimless crime, right?

"I would." The finality in his voice told me he'd made up his mind.

My heart dropped, and I closed my eyes to keep from crying. "Regardless, I want you to know you've made me happy."

I wanted him to know the truth. "Kidnapping you and spending these past days with you have been the happiest of my life. I don't want you to ever regret your decision. You've given me a gift I never expected to receive… a chance to experience the type of future I might've had, if not for the cards I was dealt."

His hands stopped moving, and I couldn't even hear him breathing.

"Please don't think I'm saying this to try to change your mind," I added, hating that I couldn't see his face.

Since I was spilling secrets, I might as well tell him everything, right? This might be my last chance. "I wanted you back then, too. You used to hang out in the park near campus and buy smoothies from the food truck I worked at. It was your laugh that first caught my attention. Then I watched how you interacted with the people around you, always quick with a kind word. It took almost a month for me to work up the courage to ask you out."

He remained silent, so I plunged ahead.

"I'd never had a crush on a guy, and my best friend had decided it was serious enough that she needed to fly across the country to offer moral support in case you turned me down." I smiled, remembering my bubbly bestie who'd threatened to tie me up and drag me to the guy if I didn't stop procrastinating.

"You have no idea how many times I practiced what I'd say to you in front of the mirror. I probably spent the same amount of brain power overthinking that as I did running my first experiment." The memory of me trying out different approaches made me laugh.

I'd practiced being seductive, aloof, and one-of-the-guys. If things hadn't taken a sharp turn, I knew I would have ended up embarrassing myself. It was kinda my thing when I was around Beckett.

My soft laughter died away as I continued my story. "She did my makeup that morning, telling me I looked so good that you wouldn't be able to turn me down. I skipped my classes, and we headed to the park to see if you'd show up. We were laughing over her dating mishaps when her face changed."

My throat tightened, and I swallowed hard. "Her eyes

glowed, and I knew she'd found her mate. I spun around, excited to see who she was looking at. It was you."

Beckett's fingers flexed on my skin, but he remained silent.

"I was so happy for her, but at the same time, I thought my soul was being ripped from my body. You two were fated to be together, and I watched with tears in my eyes as she rushed into your arms." I pressed fingers to my burning eyes.

"Once I knew she wasn't going to be rejected, I left the park. I spent the day sobbing until I had no tears left to cry. But by the time she returned to my townhouse that night, I'd wiped them away and was ready to celebrate with her. She was horrified when she realized you were the man I'd fallen for, but I assured her that a silly crush was nothing compared to a fated mate. Heck, I almost convinced myself.

"Idrie was like a sister to me, and her happiness mattered more than my own. I loved knowing she had a good mate, and after that first night, we never spoke about what I'd felt for you. Those were emotions I locked away forever."

The only reason I'd caved to his touch in the hotel was because he'd caught me at a weak moment... when he'd literally caught me in his arms as I'd passed out.

I remembered the day I'd lost Idrie as if it had happened yesterday. We were walking and talking... then suddenly she was gone. The car had been going so fast that it caused a gust of wind that ripped at my hair and clothing as it sped by.

I could still hear the sickening crunch of her body as it took the full impact of the car, then the heavy thud as she hit the ground. I could still feel the raw pain in my throat as I screamed her name until I couldn't do more than whisper for days.

Beckett had appeared out of nowhere, racing to her side with an inhuman speed that would put world-class sprinters to shame. What came after was a blur in my mind, but I remembered EMTs arriving, the sheet covering her still body after they took her from Beckett, and the ambulance taking her away.

He'd gone into shock, and I knew I couldn't leave him there. I led him home and had seen the moment his eyes went blank, as if he wasn't really there anymore. I'd washed away the blood, trying to reach him in whatever depths he'd vanished into. Not out of any romantic ideas or feelings, but simply because he was the last link to Idrie that I had... and she was the only family I'd ever known.

But just like everyone else in my life, he'd disappeared, and I'd been alone.

Shaking my head to clear away the memories, I realized he still hadn't moved. With great effort, I pushed up on my elbows and twisted my torso so I could see his face and make sure he was okay.

"I'm sorry I left you that night." He ground out the words, and there was no denying the pain behind them. "I wasn't me anymore."

It was as though he'd heard the thoughts I'd kept to myself.

"We all handle grief differently, and that was a long time ago," I assured him. "Besides, I haven't been myself the past few days either. I'm sorry for disrupting your life with my problems."

Scooting out from beneath him, I pushed to my feet and headed to find my laptop. I'd done enough dreaming over what could never be. It was time to get back to work on my cure, and he needed to get back to his pack.

As wonderful as the brief reprieve had been, it was over.

CHAPTER 14

Beckett

She'd accepted my answer with grace, which is what I'd wanted. Right?

So why did it hurt to feel her pulling away from me? How else had I expected this to end?

I needed to get back to my pack.

But the consuming ache in me rose up like an insurmountable tide. Just minutes ago, she'd been beneath me with my hands stroking her tight muscles. I wanted her more than I'd ever remembered wanting a woman, and it was tearing me up inside that I could feel her withdrawing.

She was trying to protect both our hearts, and probably didn't want to make me feel bad for my decision, but I hated the fact that she was going to walk away from me.

No, I was the one walking away. Just like I'd done in the past.

She'd left the room, but her hurt still lingered in the air like the scent of smoke—sharp and acrid.

There was no way I could explain my actions without giving away a secret that would give humanity the key to wiping out my species. All humans had to do in order to fragment our packs and drive our wolves mad was to kill some of our mates. And that information in the wrong hands could devastate my kind.

I was selfish if I let Lilou die before her work was launched into the world, which would cause the deaths of many that her research could have saved.

I was selfish if I betrayed the oaths I'd taken to protect my species by revealing the secret that could destroy everyone I'd sworn to protect.

I was selfish if I followed my heart and claimed the purple-haired beauty who hadn't simply captured my body, but who had also captured my heart.

There was no answer that would do right by everyone, and I knew I'd live with countless *what ifs* for the rest of my life.

I stretched out on the couch, staring up at the rough plank ceiling. She returned to the living room, settling in the armchair by the window. The minutes ticked by as her fingers raced over the laptop's keys, her attention solely on the screen.

"Thank you, for everything," she said in an upbeat tone, but sadness laced her words.

I could hear the coming goodbye and I wasn't ready for that, even though I knew the decision wasn't mine to make.

"Thank *you*," I responded, hating the formality of the words.

Just a few hours ago, I'd been pleasuring her in intimate ways, and now we sounded like coworkers—or strangers.

She took a sip of water, then spoke again. "I think it's time we go our separate ways."

I sensed that was the opposite of what she truly wanted, but I understood she needed to focus on her work. Her life force was slowly draining from her worn-down body.

No matter how much I wanted to harden my heart against the truth, Lilou was nearing the end. Based on the changes to her body and scent I'd observed since being pushed inside her vehicle, she had a matter of a week or two left... and that was being optimistic.

She was going to die. And if I bit her, we'd both die because I couldn't come back from losing another mate. I wouldn't have cared to die alongside her, but I was an alpha, and I had given my word that I would protect my pack.

So maybe she was right. Parting ways might be the best bet.

"I don't want that," I said, deciding to give her the same honesty she'd given me.

From across the living room, she closed her laptop. Shifting in her seat, she pulled a knee to her chest and rested her chin on it. Her eyes were a dull violet as they watched me.

She was so beautiful, yet so fragile, and I longed to gather her in my arms and never let her go.

"I don't either, but I don't know what other options we have." She lifted both of her shoulders.

Vulnerability shimmered in her eyes, and even though I hadn't marked her, I felt the pull of the mate bond demanding that I protect her.

But she wasn't my responsibility. My pack was my responsibility and where my loyalty was supposed to lie.

This should have been an easy call.

I couldn't mark her.

This wouldn't work.

We needed to part ways.

The end.

But everything inside me struggled against that reality.

Standing, I approached her. Lilou's gaze followed my movements, but otherwise she remained still.

Defeat and fatigue were etched on her face, making me question my choices once again. I kneeled in front of her. I fought the urge to reach out and touch her, but I kept my hands to myself.

"I'm sorry. I really do feel awful—"

She lifted a hand, interrupting my words. "You have nothing to apologize for. I'm the one who messed up. I shouldn't have kidnapped you or tried to push you to do this."

I almost snorted, but restrained myself. Did she truly believe I'd stayed because she'd kidnapped me? I could've left at any time. She was incredible in countless ways, but she utterly sucked at being a kidnapper. But I wasn't going to point that out.

"I'm glad you did, and I've enjoyed our time together."

Her lips pressed together in a flat smile that didn't reach her eyes. "It was nice to see you again."

"You're an amazing woman. What you're doing is incredible and selfless." I reached out to cup her cheek, and she blinked in surprise.

The warmth of her skin seeped into my palm, and I almost regretted that I'd touched her. It definitely didn't make things easier for either of us. But I couldn't bring myself to pull away. I could swear I sensed an invisible thread pulling us closer to one another.

"I want you in every possible way," I admitted.

Her gaze locked with mine and she studied me, as if searching for the truth. This time, a smile lit up her face and the storm clouds in her eyes lifted.

She reached out, running her fingers across my jaw. My wolf pushed forward, and I struggled to rein in the beast.

"Thank you for saying that." The shyness in her voice only increased my desire for her. "I want you in every possible way too, and I do understand why you can't mark me."

"I appreciate that, but trust me, you don't know. It's a…" My heart squeezed. "The price is much higher than you know."

"You don't owe me an explanation," she assured me, gently patting my knee before pulling her hand back.

"It's funny, really." She wrapped both arms around her

leg, a faraway look crossing her face. "You'd do anything to save your pack. We're the same, you and I. I'd do anything to protect countless lives. Even give up the little bit of time I have left here."

She was right. I'd give my life in a heartbeat to protect my pack, just as she was willing to do the same for humanity.

Maybe I was making the wrong choice.

Someone would step up to lead the pack for me when I was gone. I'd hoped to protect my people for a long time, but fate had a funny way of messing up our plans.

I wasn't afraid of sacrifice.

But I was terrified of experiencing the pain of losing another mate. And I hated that I'd be forcing one of my own to put me down like a rabid animal. There was nothing pretty about a feral wolf, and putting one down came with significant risk.

"You're a better person than I." That was the truth of the matter. "You're willing to give up everything to help the world."

Her smile turned sad, but she didn't say anything more. She stood up, her movements slow and unsteady.

Concern flashed through me, and I rose with her, catching her arm just above the elbow. She leaned into me for a moment, her sweet scent wrapping itself around me.

"What are you doing?" I asked, my voice husky and barely above a whisper.

She pulled away and glanced up at me. "You're hungry again. Feeding you is a full-time job."

"You don't need to feed me," I protested.

"After we eat, I'll pack my things and we'll head back to your pack." She tossed the words over her shoulder as she disappeared into the kitchen.

I stood still, wanting nothing more than to stride into the kitchen, pick her up, and carry her back out to the couch. She shouldn't be wasting her energy on me. Her work was going to require every last bit of the precious energy she had left.

A thought hit me with the force of a freight train.

If I couldn't mark her, maybe I could help her.

I didn't know the first thing about her work, but I could be moral support, keep her fed and make sure she stayed hydrated. If she allowed it, I could be a sounding board and act as her assistant, making things easier for Lilou through the last stages of her work.

"What if I help you?" I asked, rounding the corner into the kitchen.

Her nose wrinkled in confusion. "What do you mean?"

"Would you consider letting me stay with you? I could go to your lab, keep you fed, hydrated, massage you when you're tense, and protect you."

She tilted her head as though seriously considering my offer. "It's a spectacularly bad idea, and we both know it."

I shrugged. "Probably."

She nodded. "I'm not too proud to admit I need help. Should I make lunch before we go?"

But I was already moving, gently pushing her from the kitchen. "I'll make lunch. You go sit and relax."

CHAPTER 15

Lilou

S itting at my desk in the lab, I read over the results again. Everything had gone exactly as I'd hoped. My drug had worked, and it had passed the most recent clinical trials.

Leaning back in my chair, I willed myself to keep it together and not burst into relieved sobs. I'd done it. Now I just needed to hang on another day or two so I could meet with the press.

Which might be a problem since each day I was able to work less and less. It was only mid-afternoon and I'd already had to lay down on the couch in my office for a nap... twice.

By the time I was ready to leave for the day, I found it difficult to drive home or prepare food. And just yesterday, I struggled to walk from the lab to my vehicle. Beckett had lifted me into his arms and carried me to the car without saying a word.

Then he'd driven us home and carried me straight to my bed. I'd fallen asleep, only waking to eat the protein rich dinner he brought to me. With my waning strength, I wouldn't have been able to work at all if it hadn't been for his attention and care.

He had declined to extend my life by biting me, yet he was willing to put aside his life to help me finish my life's work. So, in reality, he'd granted my request, just not in the way I'd asked.

I hated knowing I was a burden, but every time I experienced guilt pangs, I reminded myself of the lives that I was trying to save.

"So what are you curing?" Beckett asked, appearing behind me.

His hands rubbed my tight shoulders, but it was his comforting warmth that helped the most at easing the soreness from my strained muscles.

"Fleas," I answered automatically.

Over the years, I'd found it was easier to make a joke than launch into a description of my work. Tilting my head back, I took in his raised eyebrows and the slight curve of his lips.

"You want to run that by me again?" he growled, the sparkle in his eyes betraying the playfulness within him.

"Do wolf shifters get fleas?" I asked, biting the inside of my cheek to keep from laughing.

Instead of answering, Beckett leaned down and kissed me.

It was unexpected, but I wasn't disappointed. He'd been a perfect gentleman during our trip from the cabin to my house the day before. And last night he'd slept in the guest room.

I'd missed snuggling into his warmth, but it was the best decision. The last thing we needed was to continue fanning the flames of desire... which was why this kiss was so unexpected.

I should've pulled away and reminded him of our arrangement—one that did not involve biting of any kind and definitely didn't include sex. Instead, I let him pull me to my feet and into his arms.

My body eagerly responded to his touch by melting against him. What if this was the last time I was able to taste his lips? Unable to resist him, I returned the kiss with pent-up enthusiasm.

He lifted me into his arms and I wrapped my legs around my waist as he pressed my back against the wall.

Beckett's tongue met mine, and I whimpered, every thought in my mind scattering like strays with a dog catcher hot on their trail. His hard length throbbed against me, and I tilted my hips, needing to feel him even if it was through several layers of fabric.

Heat flooded every nerve ending in my body as his mouth and hands grew aggressive and demanding. His lips trailed down the column of my neck, and his hands slid under my shirt to explore my flushed skin. A moment later, he sat me on my desk and kneeled in front of me.

"I don't think…" My words trailed off as my mouth went dry.

I wasn't sure what he had planned, and while I wanted him—and wanted this—I still wasn't sure that intimacy between us was a good idea.

Not to mention, this was going to be a late night in the lab as I prepared for my presentation. I wasn't sure I had the energy to spare.

"Don't take this the wrong way, but I'm, um… running on a low battery right now."

He pulled me against his powerful chest and I was amazed at how being in his arms felt like being home. Inhaling deeply, I snuggled into his heat.

"Shh." Beckett ran a hand down my hair, gently shushing me.

"Are you trying to tell me to be quiet?" I asked, pretending to be incensed.

"For someone with low energy, you sure are spicy." His mouth captured mine in a gentle kiss, then traveled down my neck.

"I really do want you." Even though I didn't owe him an explanation, I didn't want him to think I was blowing him off.

"And I want you," he rumbled.

With him nuzzling my neck, it was hard to think. But then a thought came into sharp focus, and I my heart leaped into my throat.

I pulled away, rolling over so that my belly pressed against the desk and my feet were on the floor. Grabbing my keyboard, I typed furiously.

Ideas were flowing freely, and I hurried to record everything as my excitement grew. When I finished, I squeezed from between the desk and Beckett's body and rushed to prepare slides according to my notes.

Adjusting the microscope, I watched, hardly daring to breathe as I waited.

There was no reaction.

"I think... I think it worked." I breathed out a sigh of relief.

Things never went that smoothly in the early phases of research, and I was thankful that for once, luck seemed to be on my side... or at least taking pity on me.

"You never did tell me what you're curing." His voice was still rough with lust, but his curiosity seemed to have won.

Exhaling, I turned to face him. "You know how transplant donors struggle with their body rejecting their new organs?"

Beckett nodded.

"I've developed a drug that has the potential to put an end to transplant rejection. Its success rate in clinical trials was over 90%."

His jaw dropped. "Are you serious? That will change the world."

"Yes, but that's not all." My body was vibrating with a chaotic mix of anxiety and excitement.

He raised a brow, waiting for me to continue.

Leaning back on the stainless-steel counter, I chose my words carefully, not sure how he would take it. "I didn't want to sway your mind. But you already decided that you're not going to mark me, so I might as well tell you."

I hesitated, swallowing hard. "You can't change your mind because of what I'm about to tell you." I didn't want him to feel guilty about changing his mind.

He lifted his hand, dragging his index finger across his heart in the universal symbol of making a promise.

My heart thumped painfully in my chest. "I discovered that my drug had the potential to cure the transfusion rejection between humans and wolves. However, I've struggled with one activating one of the components due to the difference in wolf and human DNA."

I could hardly force the words out past my raw, aching throat. "And I'm pretty confident I just figured out the last part of the formula. I won't live to see it through all the testing and trials, but using my notes, a cure can be developed within a few years."

Pain flashed across his face, and my stomach dropped.

We were both remembering Idrie. The EMTs had said that her femoral artery had been nicked. They'd told us she'd lost too much blood already, and she was slipping into unconsciousness. Then they couldn't find her pulse at all.

Deep down, I knew that even if they'd gotten her to the hospital before she passed away, they wouldn't have stocked enough of the blood her body would've been able to accept.

The feeling of helplessness I'd experienced that night had lingered for several years. It had driven me to research the challenges wolves faced when it came to medical care.

Depending on the severity of the wounds, most wolves could heal themselves within hours. But they couldn't replenish their blood fast enough to keep from bleeding out, which was why blood transfusion was the number one issue wolves faced. They couldn't accept human blood... but my drug was going to change that.

"You are working to save the lives of humans... and wolves?" Beckett asked, his voice hoarse.

I nodded, then gripped the table as I tried to stop the world from spinning. My heart pounded harder and faster until I couldn't hear anything over the thundering in my ears.

"I didn't want to tell you, because..." I faltered as the edges of my vision darkened. Focusing on his blurry form, I drew strength from knowing I wasn't alone. "Because..."

No, no, no. This can't be happening! I just need one more day.

My stomach heaved, and I fought to keep from throwing up my lunch. Everything went silent and my exhausted body finally caved.

My fight was over and the cursed mutation had won.

I WOKE UP, alone.

Heart pounding, I sat up, looking around in confusion. I was in my bedroom, but I had no memory of how I'd gotten there.

"Beckett?" I called, searching the dimly lit room but finding it empty.

An internal tug had me looking to my right, and I felt certain he was somewhere in that direction, but all I could see was the far wall of my bedroom and the empty chair by the window.

Sitting up, I was stunned to realize energy was flowing through me, making me feel as though I could leap from the bed and do all the things I hadn't been able to do for years.

I clambered from my bed, gasping in shock at the absolute lack of pain or faintness in my body. No, that wasn't true. A deep pain thrummed in my chest, and I felt almost desperate to find Beckett.

What if I was having a heart attack? Was I going to die alone?

Closing my eyes, I steadied my breathing so I could take stock of my body and search for what hurt. But other than that hollow ache, nothing else in my body was causing me pain.

I was alive, energized, and ready to take on the world. Scrubbing a hand down my face, I froze as his scent filled my lungs as though my nose was pressed against his skin. Bringing my fingertips to my lips, I gasped as I realized I was smelling where he'd touched me.

Dazed, I stared around the room, taking in the sharp colors as my ears rang from the noise all around me. I'd been living in a two-dimensional world, trapped in a flat, boring, unimpressive existence. But now I could hear, smell, taste, even feel the world around me as though it were a living thing.

And with a flash of clarity, I understood why. My fingers brushed my neck, confirming what I already knew.

He did it.

Beckett had promised he wouldn't, but he'd marked me… then he'd left me alone.

CHAPTER 16
Beckett

Staring out the taxi window, I told myself I wasn't going to give myself time to wonder if I'd done the right thing or not. Thankfully, the driver had nothing to say, and simply glanced at me occasionally in the rearview mirror.

I was on my way back to my pack, wanting to ensure everything was running smoothly. But that was only part of the reason.

The real reason was that I needed to give myself time to adjust to the initial draw that came from marking a mate.

It was a miracle I'd been able to pull myself away before she'd awakened, and I'd caved to my desire. I desired her so wholly that I feared I would do more to her than she was ready to handle.

I'd return to her, but I wondered if I could survive being away. Because being separated from her felt as though I had a deep gash in my chest and the stitches were being pulled out of the fresh wound.

My eyelids drifted closed, and I was back in the lab and watching Lilou crumple. I'd vaulted forward, scooping her up into my arms before she could hit the ground.

I'd caught her... barely.

For a horrifying moment, I thought she'd died, but then I caught the faint sound of her stuttering heartbeat.

Right then, I'd made my decision. I didn't care about research, obligations, or responsibilities. All that mattered was keeping her with me for as long as possible. I wasn't ready to say goodbye.

She was mine.

My wolf lunged forward, taking control, and I'd let him. My teeth had sunk into Lilou's almost gray skin and claimed her as mine.

Instinct had taken over, but I'd managed to curb the side-effect of claiming a mate, although it had taken an insane amount of effort—effort I was still paying for.

But knowing she was alive and as well as she could be made it all worth it.

And Lilou had gotten what she wanted—more time to continue her research and save lives.

My phone buzzed, and I lifted the device. *Where are you staying tonight?*

Oliver might be suspicious about why I'd taken an unplanned leave of absence, and what I'd been up to, but I would tell him everything once I got back. He was my right hand and my best friend.

If anyone in my pack had a problem with me marking her, I'd fight them to the death. Her research would help humans and wolves alike, and if that wasn't a good enough reason for them to accept me, they could bite me... on the arse.

I'd already covered her tracks so she wouldn't face retribution from the pack for kidnapping me. Besides, I doubted they would ever believe the tiny human female could have held me captive if I'd wanted to be free.

Suddenly exhausted, I realized I wasn't ready to answer questions, especially when I was struggling with the pull of the mate bond. Sagging against the seat, I glanced out the window and spotted a sign for a hotel.

Green Gardens Inn, I texted Oliver, then lowered my phone to my lap and asked the driver to stop at the inn. The driver glanced at me in the mirror, then turned into the parking lot and dropped me at the front door.

I thanked him and opened the app on my phone to leave a five-star review, thankful for the silent ride. With a wave, he drove off, and I headed for the glass front door of the brick-faced inn.

Pushing open the door, I saw the woman behind the counter shake her head. "Sorry, sir. We have no vacancy. Some group is in town for a convention, so we're totally booked."

"Thanks," I responded, heading back out the door and blowing out a long breath.

Every molecule in my body was tugging me toward my mate, but I continued to resist it. I could only hope that as a human, she wasn't experiencing the same level of agony I was.

With a brisk stride, I headed down the street toward another motel. It was a slightly seedier looking place, but maybe they'd have room. My whole world had been turned upside down, and I needed to ground myself.

Turning on the paved walkway, I made my way to the front door of the motel. All the while, my mind flashed with images of the time I'd spent with Lilou. I wished more than anything she was by my side now, making her light-hearted comments and infusing humor into every moment.

Pushing the door open, I headed toward the counter. "Room for one, please."

The older man behind the counter nodded his gray head. "That'll be a hundred for the night. Check out at eleven a.m."

I opened my wallet and pulled out cash.

"Not going to ask for my ID and name?" I asked.

Wasn't it a legal requirement for him to gather that information?

The old man winked. "As far as I'm concerned, you're Willie B. Hardigan."

I laughed, and took the key from him.

"Room three. Enjoy your stay, Willie." He turned his attention back to his phone, no doubt doom scrolling some social media platform.

We were all addicted to the mini dopamine hits. But as I

headed for the door, I realized how little time I'd spent on my phone when I'd been with Lilou.

I'd been present. No need to escape. No desire to lose myself for a few moments. I'd just wanted to be with her.

Opening the green door, I stepped into my room. At least the place smelled clean—like bleach and laundry detergent. Locking the door behind me, I made my way to the bed and dropped down on the corner.

My mind drifted to my pack. They wouldn't dare harm my mate. And anyone who tried something stupid would be swiftly put in their place.

I rubbed my chest, trying to ease the hollow ache. My heart was tugging me toward her, as if I'd forgotten that I'd left half my soul behind.

Closing my eyes, I envisioned her smile, her adorable sense of humor, the hesitant look in her eyes right before I kissed her, and the way she fit so perfectly in my arms. I remembered the first shower and the way she'd trusted me.

Somehow, I didn't think the mate bond was the reason I felt so empty and alone.

I lay back on the bed. My duty was with my pack. I needed to make sure everything was running smoothly, and set up provisions in my absence. Because I wasn't going to waste a single minute of the life she had left.

But with each second that passed, I found myself tempted to turn my back on them and hunt her down. I wanted to send her a message, but I'd promised myself I'd give her space to adjust to being marked without having to deal with an alpha wolf desperate to claim her body with more than just a bite.

She might be mad at me when she realized that marking her, meant death for me when she succumbed to her illness, but I'd been helpless to let her go.

Exhaustion settled over me, and I drifted off into that place between wakefulness and dreams.

She approached me, her brow creased. "You left."

"I did what I had to do to protect you," I said, watching her as she circled me.

She lifted a shoulder. "Or you're protecting yourself."

Maybe I was. What I felt for her was unfamiliar, all-consuming, and terrifying.

"You should come back to me." Everything about her was alluring, from her voice, to her smile, to her almost catlike movements.

Jerking awake, I blinked at the stained ceiling. I'd forgotten about the dreams. The mated wolves said they were like a siren's call, trying to drag us together despite my worries. It was new territory for me, and the dream overwhelmed me, dragging me back below the surface.

Her lips captured mine, and my body hardened. "You're mine now."

With a growl, I try to shoo away dream Lilou.

She giggled. "Don't think you can escape me now."

I didn't want to escape... I just needed to keep space between us to ensure her safety. But I felt myself sinking into the haze, pulled in by her scent, her heartbeat, her delicate smile. Lost in the dream, I watched her strip down and level a *come and get me* smile in my direction.

The lines between reality and dreamscape blurred as I dropped my inhibitions and stalked toward her. I couldn't hurt this dream version of her, and I sure as heck couldn't fight my desire for her any longer.

An odd scent permeated the dream as I chased her down—something familiar, thick, choking. But the dream dragged me deeper into sleep and my grasp on reality grew tenuous.

"Come with me," she whispered, appearing in my arms, her gaze trapping me in a way that promised she'd never let me go. That was exactly what I wanted.

But an acrid scent clogged my throat, and I coughed.

"Don't go," she whispered, her lips touching mine. "Don't leave me."

"Never again," I whispered, giving myself over to the dream.

CHAPTER 17

Lilou

From my hiding spot backstage, I peered out at the crowd gathered in the auditorium to celebrate my work. Flashes flickered from cameras around the darkened room, and the red lights glowed as reporters began recording.

This was the moment I'd waited for—I was going to present my research and put it out into the world where it could hopefully be used to save countless lives.

After being left alone the day before, I'd felt too good to rest. I dressed quickly and returned to my lab. The first thing I'd done was draw my blood and compare it to the results from my last blood panel.

To my shock, almost all my values were within normal ranges. There were a couple of things I'd need to recheck, but if the blood test was to be trusted, my organs were no longer failing.

If this wasn't just a temporary fluke due to the bite, it meant I might live. And that was something I hadn't dared to let myself even consider as an option.

But how was Beckett going to feel about being stuck with me for life if he couldn't even handle staying with me the night he'd marked me? A fling was one thing... a lifetime commitment was another.

Pushing those anxiety-inducing thoughts from my mind, I'd poured my energy into going over the results of all the recent tests my drug had gone through and prepared my presentation.

All that was left was presenting it to the world so further trials and research could continue, and drug companies could start the race to see who could be first to manufacture it for the public.

By giving my complete research to the world, I was forcing the companies to compete with each other, rather than one company being allowed to gate-keep it. I hoped that would keep the cost of the drug in reasonable ranges.

This was the day I'd prayed I would survive long enough to see. But as I scanned the sea of faces, instead of feeling elated, icy discomfort flooded my veins.

When I'd emailed the organizer at two this morning with confirmation that I was ready to share the results of my research, I'd expected it to take weeks for her to put together a press event.

She'd emailed me four hours later with instructions to

arrive at the auditorium by eight in the morning. I'd kept her in the loop over the last month, but I couldn't believe she'd gathered this crowd in a matter of hours.

I was impressed, but I was also frustrated. In every chat I'd had with her over the past few weeks, I'd been clear I had no desire to be recognized.

I'd wanted a smaller private event without cameras where I could answer candid questions and the focus could be solely on the research. Heck, I'd even asked if we could have someone else present the research for me, but she'd brushed that off.

What had Carol said? *This is a good way to establish trust with people by putting a face to your research and hard work.*

When I'd fired back that I didn't need or want to be recognized for my work, I just wanted to help people, she'd merely smiled and put her hand on mine.

Ignoring my requests, she'd turned the announcement into a headline-grabbing event. Like it or not, I'd have to go through with it. My stomach churned, and I flattened my palm against it.

I took a deep breath, trying to calm my racing heart, but coughed as the acrid scent of smoke filled my nose. The thread pulling me toward my mate caused my heart to jerk, and a sense of dread settled over me.

Carol stepped to my side; her blonde hair and makeup were perfectly styled, a contrast to the messy bun I'd pulled my tangled purple mane into. At least the dark bruises under my eyes had vanished and my skin had a bit of color.

For a moment, I wondered if she was planning to go

over my opening lines one more time before things got underway.

"You seem tense. Is there anything I can do to help put you at ease?" she asked in that calm voice I'd focused on during our previous interactions.

I might not always like *what* she said, but I did like *how* she said it.

Sniffing the air, I tried to figure out if I really was smelling smoke or if it was a weird side effect of the bite.

"Do you smell smoke?" I asked.

Her eyebrows drew together, and concern filled her brown eyes. "I don't smell anything burning. You're probably stressed and experiencing some stage jitters. Did you get any sleep last night? I've told you that you have to take care of yourself. You can't keep burning the candle at both ends."

Burning the candle at both ends? No, over the past few months, I'd practically lit the entire thing on fire and roasted marshmallows over it. Rest and self-care weren't high priorities when I could feel my life essence fading.

She flashed her brilliant white smile, but her calm demeanor did nothing to ease my worry. If anything, the tension within me escalated, gathering traction with every passing moment as I shifted my weight from one foot to the other.

My body was screaming at me to run before it was too late. Too late for what, though?

The overwhelming sense of foreboding was so powerful

that sweat broke out across my forehead and darkness unfurled along the edges of my vision.

I wasn't experiencing stage fright, I was fighting full blown terror.

"You don't look so good." Carol's pretty face blurred.

Yeah, well, I didn't feel so good, either.

No matter how many times I tried to convince myself I was just experiencing nerves because I didn't like being the center of attention, I couldn't escape the clutches of my anxiety.

"I can get you a sick bag if you're going to throw up," she offered.

My pulse thundered in my throat and my lungs deflated, making it impossible to suck in a full breath. The acrid sting of smoke caused my throat to constrict painfully, and I began to cough.

Carol reached out and touched my shoulder. "Are you okay?"

Her words sounded distorted and far away, as if I was drowning and she was speaking from above the surface of the water.

"I... I can't breathe," I gasped.

This wasn't jitters or nerves. This felt like I was dying.

A tsunami of fear and sorrow rose above me, threatening to crush me beneath its overwhelming weight. Unable to stand it for another second, I rushed away, blindly searching for the exit.

I wished Beckett were there. He'd know how to calm me.

As I thought of the handsome alpha wolf, my fear intensified, and with an audible snap in my mind, I suddenly knew what was happening. My body, brain, and heart were warning me that Beckett was in danger.

My mate needed me.

"Lilou!" Carol yelled, her heels clicking as she chased me down a seemingly endless beige hallway.

"My assistant is in the crowd. She will give the presentation!" I shouted over my shoulder as I raced toward the exit.

"You can't leave!" she shrieked, her calm exterior cracking slightly as she realized her perfect press release wasn't going to go how she'd planned.

Additional footfalls echoed around me, warning me she wasn't the only one giving chase. Muffled voices were followed by a shocked yelp. I never slowed as I picked up my pace, leaving them behind me.

My lungs burned, my body ached, and my mind raced. Beckett was in trouble; I could feel it in my bones. Bursting out into the back alley, the terror clawed at my chest like a living thing seeking an escape.

I latched onto the desperate feeling. Beckett needed me, and I was going to do whatever it took to save him. I refused to let him die.

Pain tore through every inch of my being, and I opened my mouth to scream in agony, but no sound came from my throat. Blazing fire seemed to be burning beneath my skin, as though my blood had been turned to gasoline and someone had lit a match.

I could feel the thing unfurling within me, shifting my very DNA to make room for itself. Collapsing onto the ground, I curled into a ball and tried to stay conscious as my skin rippled and my heart stuttered.

When the pain finally vanished, I lay still with my eyes closed. A symphony of scents assaulted my nose, and I fought the urge to cover my ears as every sound in the city seemed to grow impossibly loud.

A cool breeze whipped down the alleyway, bringing with it the faint scent of fire.

Beckett.

Scrambling to my feet, I wobbled, then glanced down. My body turned to stone as I caught sight of two large gray paws.

I'd shifted.

That had been the cause of the pain. His words echoed in my mind. *If I bite you and you turn, you'll die.*

He was right. Wolves had unique DNA that allowed their bodies to accommodate the shift. Those who were cursed with the mutation had a trapped wolf inside them. If we shifted, releasing the inner beast, our human body was damaged beyond repair, becoming unstable.

Despite knowing I was still going to die, all I could think was how ticked off Beckett was going to be when he found out.

Well, then maybe he shouldn't have left me unattended. Last time that happened, I'd kidnapped an alpha, so we both knew I couldn't be trusted to make the best decisions.

I guessed the universe had seen fit to give me one last

chance to do some good with my short life. Peace settled over me. My research was in good hands, and as long as I could save Beckett, I would accept my death gracefully.

I began to run, my movements wooden at first, but by the time I reached the end of the alley, I'd found my stride.

I soaked in every bit of information around me and focused on the thin sliver of invisible silk thread that tethered me to my mate.

Racing toward him, I became one with the wind. I rushed across busy roads, barely noticing the screeching tires and blaring horns. My paws thundered against the pavement as I darted between alleys and jumped fences as I made my way toward the center of my universe.

My mate.

My love.

Nothing else mattered but making sure he was safe.

By shifting, I'd condemned myself to almost certain death, but I couldn't think of any better way to repay him for caring for me through the last days of my research than to save him. A life for a life. It was fair.

I would have loved to listen as the world learned of the capabilities of the drug I'd developed and the doors of possibility it opened for future research. By building off my research, I suspected a cure could be developed for those who suffered from immune conditions caused by their body attacking itself. Hearing the gasps and murmur of excitement as medical history was forever changed was something I'd dreamed of for years.

My research had been the most important thing in my life. But that had changed.

The cure would save lives with or without me—that was kind of the point.

But it was Beckett who truly needed me.

I knew I'd made the right choice. It was the only one I could happily live—or die—with.

CHAPTER 18
Beckett

I peered out the window, staring at the hotel across the street and watching the flames lick the sky. Two carefully positioned fire trucks battled the blaze as countless cops, EMS workers, and random people milled about, their tense faces covered in soot.

My dreams had been filled with thoughts of my mate, and I'd slept through most of the chaos. It wasn't until the wind shifted and sent smoke directly toward my hotel that I'd awakened. We hadn't been ordered to evacuate, but I'd watched as guests poured out into the parking lot, dragging their luggage behind them.

Focusing back on the roaring fire across the street, I couldn't believe I'd almost stayed there last night. If they hadn't been full, I would have been caught in that blaze. The minor inconvenience of the previous day had become the event that may very well have saved my life today.

My phone dinged with a message and I lifted the device to read the words. *The fire is on the news. Please tell me you're okay!*

Oliver's message struck something deep within me and I realized with shock that my pack likely thought I was dead.

I'm fine. I stayed at the place across the street. I'm looking at the fire right now. I snapped a picture and sent the image along with my message.

He'd mentioned this being on the news, so I turned on the TV in my room, trying to ignore the suffocating scent of smoke. On TV, a newsperson spoke in worried tones about the high likelihood of casualties as the burning hotel came into frame behind them.

High likelihood of casualties.

That phrase sent a shiver down my spine. I didn't want to think about how narrowly I'd escaped death.

"Authorities aren't sure what started the fire, but preliminary findings suggest a blown transformer may have sparked the blaze." The news woman's eyes widened, and she spun around as the roof of the hotel collapsed with a crash that was deafening.

My room shook, and I hurried to the window and glanced out. The heat of the flames had devoured most of the building, leaving a pile of blackened wooden bones in its wake. My heart sank as I recalled the words of the clerk who'd turned me away.

We have no vacancy. Some group is in town for a convention or something, so we're totally booked.

I wanted to rush over and offer help to any possible survivors, but I knew I'd only be in the way. It was best to let the professionals handle things, and acting on impulse would be a good way to get myself killed—or worse, put others at risk. But that didn't stop the sadness I felt by standing there doing nothing.

A car whipped into the parking lot, catching my attention. To my surprise, Oliver exited the vehicle and walked into the office. He looked calm and relaxed, no doubt relieved to know I wasn't dead and he wasn't going to be forced into the alpha role.

I also knew he wouldn't find me, because the man behind the counter had checked me in under a bogus name. And with the heavy stench of smoke, I didn't expect his sense of smell to lead him to my door.

My first instinct was to step out and call his name, but something held me still. Instead, I watched with a sinking stomach as the building across the street collapsed in on itself the rest of the way while firefighters aimed streams of water to douse the flames.

You're not here. Oliver's message jolted me out of my thoughts.

I am. Room three. I sent the message and watched as he exited the office and headed in the direction of my room.

I opened the door for him and stepped back. Oliver practically stormed inside, slamming the door shut and locking the deadbolt behind him.

"If you want something done right, do it yourself," he said, putting his hands on his thighs just above his knees and leaning forward as if winded.

I didn't understand what he meant by the comment.

"You are my best friend and right-hand man. I trust you to run the pack while I'm gone," I said, assuming he meant that I needed to deal with the pack myself.

He shook his head, taking a deep breath. "You don't understand." With a wave of his hand, he gestured to the window. "That fire wasn't an accident."

When he straightened and met my eyes, I saw no warmth in his glowing brown orbs.

The hair on my body stood on end and my blood turned to icy slush. "What are you talking about? The news said—"

He chuckled, running a hand through his tawny hair. "The news thinks exactly what we wanted them to think."

With another wave of his hand, he motioned me to the chair at the desk. I sat down, sensing something wasn't quite right but struggling to reconcile the unhinged man in front of me with my steady as a rock beta.

Details that now seemed to be sliding into place like keys unlocking a door, even though my thoughts seemed unable to wrap around the entirety of them. Had Oliver lost his mind? Had the pressures of leading broken him?

"Don't even think about doing anything stupid," he

said, pulling out a gun and a pair of handcuffs. "Put these on," he ordered, leveling the gun at my face.

I had a 50/50 shot of dodging the bullet. Reluctantly, I fastened the cuffs around my wrist. Keeping the gun steady, he moved forward and pulled a chain from his pocket, which he used to fasten my cuffs to the chair.

The cuffs and chain wouldn't do more than slow me down if I wanted to break free, but as long as he had the gun pointed at my face, Oliver definitely had the advantage.

"What are you doing?" I asked, worried he'd lost his mind even as the truth began to sink in.

"Getting rid of you," he said with a shake of his head, as if he couldn't believe I was too stupid to figure out his master plan.

He pressed the gun to my head. "See, I love leading the pack. I'd been trying to find a way to take your place as alpha for the past two years. Lady luck must love you, because you were supposed to die the night you disappeared. Hired killers were waiting to ambush you as you walked to the meeting. When you didn't show up for the meeting, I thought I'd finally won."

The coldness in his voice left no doubt that he was being honest. "But then I got the text saying you were a no show. You managed to disappear without a trace. I hoped maybe you'd gone loco again, but then you just had to pop back up."

"What happened to you?" I breathed, moving to stand, but stopping when he waved the gun at me.

"You were supposed to die in that fire! It would have been so tidy and without any pesky loose threads. The pack would mourn your tragic passing and I'd step up and run things the way they should've been run. The way you were never strong enough to lead."

Narrowing my eyes, I studied the man I'd considered a brother, but who I'd never truly known. My heart grew heavy at the betrayal of someone I thought had my back through thick and thin.

In true villain fashion, he continued rambling about his plan. Was he trying to flaunt his genius to have me acknowledge how smart he was? Why didn't he just get on with what he'd come here to do?

His words came to an abrupt halt, and he inhaled. "You claimed a mate. That's why you ran off, isn't it? To get laid. Weren't there enough pack females always throwing themselves at you?"

"We've been friends forever," I said, trying to connect with him, but unwilling to answer any questions about Lilou.

"You're a fool. You should've ruled with an iron fist, not a gentle hand." He moved the curtain an inch to check the fire across the street.

"I want my pack to follow me because they trust my judgments to be fair and they respect me, not because they fear me." I never wanted to lead with force.

Alphas were meant to be protectors, not dictators.

Oliver continued his rant as if I hadn't spoken. "I'm going to do what you should have done all along. Under my rule, the pack is going to grow, establish more ground, and take what's ours."

My throat tightened. "You're going to start a war."

"I'm going to do what you were too weak to do," he spat.

"You killed innocent people in that hotel!" The heart-wrenching betrayal I'd felt quickly shifted to a blinding rage.

He shrugged. "Humans. They don't really count."

"They don't count? They have just as much right to life as we do!" My muscles flexed as I tested my restraints. "And how many wolves will die because of your greed if you try to take another pack's land?"

"I'm the alpha now, and I will make what sacrifices are necessary to ensure my pack prospers." He claimed the title so confidently, as if he simply expected me to agree and bow before him.

"It takes more strength to lead with kindness and do what's right than to try to rule with fear." I knew I couldn't talk him out of his crazed mindset, but I needed to stall him while I planned an attack.

He rolled his eyes. "That's what weak wolves tell themselves to cover up their inadequacies."

I opened my mouth to respond, then closed it as I caught a familiar sweet scent.

Lilou.

I'd hardly registered her name, before a dark shape hurtled into the double-paned window behind him and shattered the glass.

Oliver turned to face the intruder, and I pushed to my feet, still attached to the chair, preparing to tackle him.

But Lilou was faster. Before I could take a single step, the dove gray wolf had launched herself at Oliver, her powerful jaws aiming for his throat.

Oliver threw up an arm, protecting his neck from her sharp teeth, but he was unable to keep himself from crashing to the ground from the impact of her body colliding with his.

She held him in place, snarling in her wolf form, still snapping at his throat. Oliver's fingers wrapped around his gun.

Summoning my alpha strength, I snapped the cuffs and blurred across the room to kick the gun from his hand with a bone-crunching thud. Then, yanking the chain free of the chair, I wound it around his wrists.

Once he was secure, I dealt him a single hard blow to the temple. His body went limp. He wasn't dead, but he would be out for a while.

Threat handled, I turned toward Lilou.

"You shifted," I whispered, my throat dry.

Her long tongue darted out to lick my cheek in what I assumed was some type of apology.

It was a miracle she'd survived at all. Her body wasn't built to handle the shift between forms. But that didn't mean she was safe.

Very few wolves who'd survived the initial shift lived very long after returning to their human form. The damage done to their bodies was simply too much.

All at once, she shifted back into her natural form, naked, trembling, and pale. Her long purple hair covered her body as she met my gaze.

"It was my turn to save you," she whispered, before her eyes rolled back and she fell forward into my arms.

CHAPTER 19

Lilou

I could feel myself fading in and out. It was as though I were lost in a maze and unable to find my way out. Then I heard Beckett's voice, and I tried to follow it. Each time he spoke, I moved closer to consciousness. *Closer to my mate.*

My eyelids seemed to be weighted down, and I groaned as I tried to open them.

"Shh. Just rest," Beckett soothed me. "Have I told you how amazing you are?" He brushed his knuckles across my cheek, leaving a trail of tingles in their wake.

Deep down, I knew it was the mate bond making him say those sweet words, but it didn't stop the butterflies from taking flight in my stomach. I opened my eyes, taking in the gorgeous man leaning over me.

"Not bad yourself." Trying to be sexy, I winked, clicked my tongue, and lifted my finger to shoot a fake finger-gun.

At Beckett's laugh, I realized I probably looked like I was suffering from a seizure.

I glanced past him at Oliver. "Does he just like to hear himself talk?" I asked. "Or is he one of those *everyone needs to worship my genius* types? I couldn't have planned my attack if he hadn't been such a blowhard."

"Don't worry about him," Beckett said. "Your body needs to rest."

"You should know I'm bad at that." Touching my mate and knowing he was safe caused the dam holding back my emotions to burst.

Unable to help myself, I pressed my palms on either side of his face and pulled his lips to mine. A lust like a raging hurricane tore through me, and I deepened the kiss, eagerly accepting anything he would give me.

"I can't believe you took on another mate," Oliver snarled, his words slightly slurred as he came to.

Beckett's chest vibrated with a vicious growl, and he broke our kiss. "You tried to kill me and take over my pack, but you're questioning *my* life choices?" Beckett traced the lines of my face as he spoke to the traitor.

"Deny it all you want, but we both know you're a weak alpha," Oliver said.

I felt for him; this jerk was his best friend—or so Beckett had thought—and here he was, betraying, lying, and trying to ruin not just Beckett's life, but his whole pack. But I hated seeing the hurt lurking in my mate's eyes.

I groaned, dropping my head back against the pillow Beckett must have placed beneath me. "And he's right back to it. Talk, talk, talk; that's all this guy does."

The sadness etched on Beckett's face eased, and the corners of his lips curved into a smile at my silliness.

As I focused on Beckett's handsome face, thinking about all the places I wished he'd put those beautiful lips, I caught a flash of movement behind him.

Faster than the speed of thought, white-hot pain sizzled through my body as my wolf took over, the intense need to protect my mate overruling all other thoughts.

Oliver lifted a knife he must have had hidden, preparing to plunge it into Beckett's back. But he was too slow.

I leaped at him, snarling in fury as I bit down on his shoulder. The cold bite of steel sliced into me like a glowing firebrand. A yelp escaped my throat, but it did nothing to distract me. My jaws clamped around his shoulder, and Oliver released the knife with a high-pitched screech of pain.

Out of the corner of my eye, I saw another wolf, and even though I'd never seen him in this form, I knew it was Beckett. My mate regarded me for a moment, his nose twitching as he glanced between my prey and me.

Lifting my head, I could feel an instinct to roll over and show him my belly in submission… which was frankly horrifying. If I was already offering myself for belly rubs, what was next? Fetch? An obsession with peanut butter? Sniffing butts?

An image of Beckett's bare, muscular butt in the shower

flashed through my mind. Maybe that wasn't the worst thing…

"She's going to die," Oliver hissed.

Beckett leaped toward his beta with a roar of fury, but Oliver managed to shift at the last second and rolled to the side. His wolf snarled and snapped at Beckett, limping slightly thanks to the damage I'd done to his shoulder.

Without warning, Oliver made a move toward me and I braced for impact since the small hotel room didn't provide a lot of space for a game of tag-you're-dead. I shouldn't have bothered, because the beta never made contact with me.

Beckett's body bowled the wolf over, sending him careening into the wall.

The second Oliver rolled to his feet, Beckett lunged forward and slammed a shoulder into him, sending him right back into the wolf-shaped dent in the drywall.

Oliver let out an angry growl and stood once more. Obviously, he didn't know when enough was enough. And maybe it was due to the mate bond, but I got the distinct impression Beckett was playing with him like a cat amusing himself with a mouse… until he grew bored and ended it with a final, killing blow.

But Beckett didn't deliver a killing blow.

The beta shifted back to human, dragging the back of his hand across his face and leaving a smear of blood across his skin.

"You will never get your pack back!" Oliver sounded very sure of himself.

It reminded me of the same way my assistant's not-quite-potty-trained youngster had petulantly shouted that she no longer needed pullups... but had been equally mistaken.

My wolf must have decided Oliver was no longer a threat, because she retreated and I returned to my human form. I fought the urge to vomit as my stomach twisted itself into knots. Being a wolf was cool, but shifting freaking sucked. Beckett remained in his wolf form, his predatory gaze never leaving his beta.

"His people need him," I retorted. "You couldn't be half the alpha Beckett is."

Oliver slowly circled Beckett, while my mate simply watched his friend-turned-adversary with an air of absolute calm.

"They did fine without him while he was getting his rocks off with you." The tone of Oliver's voice and the way his gaze traveled my naked body made me feel like I needed a scalding shower.

My fingers twitched, longing to yank a sheet from the bed to cover myself. But somehow, I sensed that would be viewed as a sign of weakness, so I lifted my chin.

I snorted, "Doubtful. Because once you've experienced the best, you never forget."

At my disrespect, Oliver forgot who was in the room. He rushed toward me, reaching for my arm... then crumbled to the floor like an overcooked gingerbread man as Beckett pounced on him.

With Beckett's paws in his back, and his sharp teeth an

inch from Oliver's throat, I wondered if I should be the one to step in.

"Do you really want to kill him?" I asked Beckett, and his feral gaze shifted to me as drool dripped from his glistening teeth to land on Oliver's face.

For a moment, he reconsidered, and I glanced at the beta, willing him to save his skin by using this opportunity to admit defeat.

Once again, he left me speechless with his inability to read a situation.

"Yes. Because if he doesn't kill me, not only will he never trust me again, but I won't rest until he is dead." Even pinned beneath an angry alpha wolf, Oliver was defiant.

My legs wobbled, and I knew I was close to losing my grip on consciousness again. Shifting had taken too much out of my still fragile body. I realized this time was different from the others when numbness spread through me, and my heart began to slow.

I met Beckett's gaze and whispered, "Protect your people."

He didn't need my permission, and I still didn't understand the rules of pack life, but I wanted him to know I wouldn't judge him for doing what had to be done to protect his pack. I had faith he'd do the right thing.

Without warning, he brought his teeth down to Oliver's throat and the sound of crunching bone filled me as my body shifted.

I stared down at my fur-covered paws, sensing the last

of my energy ebbing from my body. My skin rippled, but thanks to the numbness, I felt no pain as my body shifted back to my trembling human form.

Something is wrong. The thought came from far away as another shift overcame me, and this time, I collapsed to the floor in my wolf form. My breathing grew shallow.

If my time had come, at least I went out doing something I could feel good about.

I'd repaid a favor.

I'd protected my pack.

I'd stood by my mate's side as we'd faced an enemy.

I'd done him proud… I hoped.

As inky darkness dragged me into unconsciousness and then far deeper than the level of dreams, I thought I heard Beckett speaking to me in that low, calming voice that filled me with peace and comfort. *Don't leave me. Without you, I'll be lost.*

The pieces clicked into place. That was the secret. Just as nothing had mattered when my mate was in danger, nothing would matter to a wolf who'd lost the other half of their soul.

By biting me, knowing I wasn't going to live long, Beckett had condemned himself to death.

He'd sacrificed himself so I could achieve my life goals.

But why would he do that when he had years to live and find someone to share his life with?

Because I only want you, my love.

CHAPTER 20
Beckett

The hotel door burst open and I glanced up into the stunned faces of three members of my pack. Their wide eyes looked from me, to Oliver's lifeless form, then at Lilou, cradled against my chest.

Her uncontrollable shifting had finally stopped, but her heartbeat was slowing and her body had gone limp. She wasn't just sleeping this time, she was dying.

Prepared for another fight, I bared my teeth in warning as Ivan stepped forward.

He froze, then dropped to his knee in a show of loyalty. "I am not a threat, Alpha."

I inhaled, tasting the air and finding only worry. He was telling the truth.

"Are you hurt?" he asked, his golden eyes locking on me.

"I'm fine."

"And your mate?" he asked as the other two began to clean up, being careful to keep their movements slow and unthreatening.

Before I could respond, someone else stepped into the room—the old man who'd been behind the counter when I'd checked in. He closed and locked the door behind him, scanning the room before meeting my gaze.

"I knew you'd be trouble," he grumbled as the hairs on the back of my neck stood on end. "You're not the only wolf to face a traitor."

He pulled a necklace from around his neck and set it on the table. With the necklace off, I could smell his wolf. Snatching the necklace from the table, he returned it to the spot near his heart under his shirt again. Once more, his scent faded to obscurity.

A wolf without a pack was a rarity. And I immediately knew who this had to be. I had only heard of this lone wolf in passing. "It's Rick, isn't it? Why did you leave your pack?

His swift exit had been a closely guarded secret of a nearby pack, and countless rumors had circulated.

Pain twisted his features. "My mate passed, and I... lost the taste for my kind... and myself."

It was a sentiment I understood better than most. As I glanced down at Lilou, and thought of the second chance at happiness she'd gifted me, I whispered, "There's still hope."

He shook his head. "Even if I wanted to, my pack would never accept me back."

I stood, cradling my love to my chest. "Mine would. You'll always have a home among us."

He'd protected me in his own way, in a way that had made it harder for Oliver to find me. Maybe if I hadn't been so blind, I could have avoided the whole mess. But I always repaid kindnesses shown to me.

Rick's expression softened. "Thank you. Now get her home. I'll clean up here."

"I can leave Vega and Gin behind." I met the gaze of the other two and they nodded in agreement.

"Sure," Rick said. "I'd appreciate that."

Turning on my heel, I left the room, following Ivan outside. He hurried to his vehicle, opening the car door for me before hurrying to his side.

I PACED BACK AND FORTH, waiting to see if she would wake. Her heart rate and breathing had stabilized, but she'd yet to open her eyes. Still, I could sense her through the mate bond. She wasn't gone.

"You're making me nervous," she mumbled, her voice heavy with sleep, "pacing like that."

I moved to her side as her eyes fluttered open and she took a moment to take in her surroundings. "Where am I?"

"My home. My room. My bed." Right where she

belonged... and where I planned to keep her for a very long time.

She must have been thinking along the same lines, because she asked, "Are we alone?"

I nodded, then sucked in my breath as her eyes began to glow a brilliant purple.

She reached for my face, and thinking she had something to tell me, I leaned close. Lilou pressed her lips to mine in a hungry kiss that set fire to my body.

I pulled back. "We can't do that now. You need to be resting."

But all traces of sleep and exhaustion were gone from Lilou's face, and the wicked sparkle in her eyes called to my body in an almost primal way. Her gaze dropped below my waist, and there was no misunderstanding what she wanted.

"Lilou, I want you. More than anything." I hated to admit it, but there was a slight pleading note in my voice.

My willpower when it came to resisting her was fading fast.

"Then show me," she purred, sucking my bottom lip into her mouth.

With a growl, I captured her mouth but fought to keep my every movement gentle. As an alpha wolf desperate to claim his mate in every way possible, it was excruciatingly painful.

Lilou gave the cutest growl and pushed me away. "Don't hold back. I'm not going to break."

Her fingers fisted the front of my shirt and pulled me back in. Our tongues met and arousal lit up every nerve ending in my body. She'd told me not to hold back, but there was no way she knew what that meant for wolves, so I reined in my desire.

"I can feel you holding back," she grumbled against my lips.

It didn't matter if she told me she was fine, I couldn't forget how fragile she'd been in my arms, or how she'd looked with our doctor stitching her up, or how I'd felt sponging her clean only hours ago. Her body had adjusted to the newly awakened beast inside her, and she'd healed faster than any of us had expected.

But it would take a long time for me to forget those hours where I'd fought to stay present with her as I waited to see if she would live or die. I couldn't allow myself to get sucked into the feral nothingness if there was a chance she would return to me.

"You were just at the brink of death. I'm not risking you any more than I already have." I didn't want her to expend more energy than she had to.

But she seemed to have other ideas. "Look, if I'm going to die soon, let me go with a smile on my face, okay? At this rate, I'll end up dying with regrets."

"Oh?" I arched a brow in question.

"I've ridden your leg, but I've never ridden the bony-pony in your pants." Her cheeks turned a deep crimson, but she held my gaze.

It was the final straw. My mate had a need and I would

eagerly meet it. Grabbing the hem of my shirt, I lifted it over my head.

Before it even hit the floor, Lilou's hands were traveling over my bare stomach and my chest. I sucked in my breath, loving her touch and wanting to feel it everywhere. Lilou wrapped her arms around my neck, rolling to her back and pulling me off balance so I nearly crushed her beneath me.

Keeping my weight on my forearms, I kissed her lips, groaning as her fingernails lightly scratched across my back, and growing far too aware of the fact that the only thing separating us were my pants and the thin sheet that pooled around her waist.

Ivan's voice filled the room, "Beckett, I—"

He released a choked, throat-clearing noise, and his embarrassment left an odor I could taste as he rapped his knuckles on the door frame.

"Not right now, Ivan," I growled against Lilou's lips.

"Of course." Ivan left the room, taking his smell with him.

She pulled away from me and smiled. "If you need to go—"

"I don't," I growled.

"Good. Because I need to come." She laughed at her own joke, and I drank in the sight and sound of my mate's happiness.

I rolled from the bed to close and lock the door, preventing any other unwanted visitors. There was nothing so important that I needed to deal with it now. The entire world could be burning, and I still wouldn't leave this room until my mate was satisfied.

When I turned around, Lilou sat naked on my bed, her glowing eyes fixed on me.

"I want you," she whispered as I closed the distance between us.

Lifting her up in my arms, I groaned as her legs wrapped around my hips, holding me close.

"I want you more," I teased, sitting on the edge of my bed with her straddling my lap.

Her weight rested on my cock, causing it to harden further. She wrapped her arms around my neck and pressed her bare skin to mine, causing both of us to shiver.

Scraping my teeth over the pulse in her neck, I felt her hips involuntarily buck forward.

"We need to get you out of these," she said, scooting off my lap and unbuttoning my slacks with shaking hands.

Her gaze met mine as she unzipped them and her pink tongue slid across her upper lip in a gesture that had my vision clouding over. She looked like a goddess, standing in front of me, the light from the window streaming in behind her and illuminating the space with splashes of sunlight.

"I love you," I whispered, meaning every word. "I tried to tell you when you were dying, and I hated myself for not telling you before it was too late.

She tensed, then relaxed, her warm breaths tickling my neck as she clung to me. "I heard you. It's why I came back."

My heart soared with happiness and I buried my nose against her neck, inhaling her scent.

"You were willing to risk losing yourself, just to give me more time." Her voice trembled. "Why?"

"Because I love you." Catching her chin in my hand, I forced her to look me in the eye. "My beautiful little mate, I started falling for you the moment you kidnapped me with a sex-toy. I've never met anyone like you, and you've turned my very black and white world into a kaleidoscope of color." Unable to resist, I lowered my mouth and teased her nipple with my tongue.

Lilou moaned, arching her back and offering me better access. "If I'd known the price you'd have to pay to mark me as your mate, I never would have asked."

"I know. And that is a secret that must be guarded." My tongue teased the hardened peak, loving the way Lilou responded to every sensation.

"I didn't want you to feel guilt, but I also didn't like making a decision when you didn't have all the information to decide what you wanted. In the end, I knew I couldn't stand by and watch you die without trying everything to save you. Even if it was a longshot."

"I didn't expect to fall for you." Her fingers threaded through my hair. "I will never forget everything you did for me. Beckett, I loved you before you marked me. Thank you for giving us a chance."

She gasped as I grabbed her hips and settled her bare heat against my throbbing erection.

"My love, an extra day with you is worth more than a

century without you," I groaned as she rocked against me. "Thank you for coming back to me."

"Mmhm," she hummed, and her eyes grew heavy with lust. "Becks, I can't wait anymore. Please."

Rolling her to her back, I lined myself up with her slick entrance. I exhaled and pressed into her heat. Our bodies fit together in a way that left no doubt in my mind that we were made for one another.

I brushed her purple hair away from her face and ran my hands from her ribs down to her hips. "You're perfect."

She smiled, placing soft kisses along my chest. "That's the mate bond talking."

But she was wrong. With her body and scent wrapped around me, and my cock buried deep inside her, I knew the mate bond was responsible for only a tiny fraction of the feelings I had toward her.

I began to move, thrusting into her silky heat and growing harder as the sounds of her pleasure filled my ears. She clung to me as though she never planned to let go as I drove us relentlessly toward our release. I watched her face, adjusting my angle and pace to ensure she was fully satisfied.

Tiny electrical currents raced up and down my arms as our bodies grew slick with sweat. There was no room for anything in my thoughts but her. Only her. Only us. Only this moment we shared.

My vision blurred, then came into focus. Glimpses of our future flashed through the bond. Lilou's eyes widened as we saw *us*; running side by side through the forest, bathing naked in a stream, coming together like two pieces of a puzzle on a moss-covered bank.

"Am I hallucinating?" she asked, her movements slowing as I continued to bury myself inside her.

"No; our mate bond allows us to see our future in snapshots," I growled, then feeling her walls tighten around me, I closed my teeth on her neck.

My fingers tangled in her hair as her hips bucked, and she screamed my name. With her body milking my length, I didn't stand a chance. Plunging deep, I held her to me as we basked in the glow of our shared love.

"I never thought about a future because I knew I couldn't have one," she panted, her body still shivering from the aftershocks of pleasure. "Now you are my future."

Capturing her mouth, I poured every bit of love into our kiss, and silently swore to make sure she always had something to look forward to.

CHAPTER 21

Lilou

I could still see the flashes of our future replaying in my mind. I'd never dared hope for a future. But now, in his arms, guided by instinct and sharing such a deeply intimate moment with him, I allowed myself to feel hope and excitement. I was going to live.

Beckett rolled to his back, pulling me on top of him, his stiff erection still deep inside me. His hands gripped my hips, and the new position had desire pooling in my belly all over again.

Leaning forward, I kissed him, loving the way his teeth nibbled my lower lip. It was almost scary how easily my body reacted to his… and how much I hungered for him.

I was deliriously happy, and for the first time in my life, hope filled me.

Hope for now.

Hope for us.

Hope for our future.

Who knew that hope could feel this intoxicating?

"Mine," Beckett growled, causing my muscles to tighten around him.

It seemed impossible, but he was already growing harder inside me. I studied my mate; the way his shoulders flexed as he guided my hips, the slight crinkles at the corners of his incredible eyes, the way stubble darkened his jaw.

"Yours," I whispered.

No matter what happened next, I'd found my love, my mate, my whole world. He'd given me the greatest gift; not just a chance to fulfill my dreams, but a chance to love and be loved. And now I would get to experience something I never thought I could... a future.

With every motion of my body, the need in my stomach wound tighter, looking for release.

His lips met mine again, and I opened my mouth for him. His tongue touched mine before swirling around in a playful way that sent sparks of pleasure cascading through me. Those sparks were followed by an explosion as I came apart.

I collapsed on his chest, my body spasming as he held me. Warmth rushed between my thighs, and I struggled to remember how to breathe.

"I've got you." His whispered assurance caused my eyes to prick with tears of joy.

He had me... and I'd never be alone again.

ABOUT DARCI R. ACULA

Darci R. Acula is Sedona Ashe's not-so-secret pen name. Sedona's books tend to focus on Reverse Harem relationships, while Darci's books feature only MF relationships.

Darci (aka Sedona) doesn't reserve her sarcasm for her books; her poor husband can tell you that her wit, humor, and snarky attitude are just part of her daily life. While she loves writing paranormal shifter reverse harem novels, she's a sucker for true love, twisted situations, and wacky humor.

Darci lives in a small town at the base of the Great Smoky Mountains in Tennessee. She and her husband share their home with their three children, adorable pup, five cats, pet arctic fox, chickens, several crazy turkeys, two chubby frogs, and over a hundred other reptiles. When she isn't working, she enjoys getting away from the computer to hike, free dive, travel, study languages, and capture images of places and animals through her photography. Darci has a crazy goal of writing a million words in a year, and spending six months exploring Indonesia.

www.darciracula.com